ACQUAINTED WITH THE NIGHT

ACQUAINTED WITH THE NIGHT ∽

by *Sollace Hotze*

CLARION BOOKS · NEW YORK

Clarion Books
a Houghton Mifflin Company imprint
215 Park Avenue South, New York, NY 10003
Text copyright © 1992 by Sollace Hotze

Library of Congress Cataloging-in-Publication Data
Hotze, Sollace
   Acquainted with the night / by Sollace Hotze.
       p. cm.
   Summary: During a summer on a Maine island, seventeen-
year-old Molly and her older cousin become very close, as she
helps him deal with his father's suicide and his experiences
in the Vietnam War, and as together they share encounters
with a troubled ghost.
   ISBN 0-395-61576-3
   [1. Cousins — Fiction. 2. Ghosts — Fiction. 3. Maine —
Fiction. 4. Islands — Fiction] I. Title.
PZ7.H8114Ac 1992
[Fic] — dc20   91-40870
                            CIP
                            AC

AGM 10 9 8 7 6 5 4 3 2 1

for Dick
who has waited long enough —
with love and gratitude

Acknowledgments

I would like to thank the Grayslake, Illinois, 1992 eighth graders who helped select the title for this book, and Laureen Scherling, who so graciously invited me into her classroom.

Thanks also to Jim Ziegler for his valuable technical assistance.

And very special thanks to Dale Griffith, who opened the shutters, and my editor, Jim Giblin, who since then has made all the difference.

*

The song lyric "Innisfree" is the poem entitled "The Lake Isle of Innisfree" by William Butler Yeats.

*

"Blowin' in the Wind" by Bob Dylan copyright © 1962 by Warner Bros. Music; copyright renewed 1990 by Special Rider Music. All rights reserved. International copyright secured. Reprinted by permission.

*

"Suzanne" copyright © 1976 by Leonard Cohen. Used by permission. All rights reserved.

*

Quotation from *Memories, Dreams, Reflections* by Carl Jung copyright © 1961. Reprinted by permission of Princeton University Press.

It is important to have a secret, a premonition of things unknown. . . . A man who has never experienced that has missed something important. He must sense that he lives in a world which is in some respects mysterious; that things happen and can be experienced which remain inexplicable. . . . The unexpected and the incredible belong in this world, and only then is life whole.

— *Carl Jung*

Author's Note

The story of Evaline Bloodsworth that unfolds in the course of the novel is based on a true story. Although I have changed the names of people and places and some of the specific details of the events, and have speculated on facts that remain unknown, the basic events of her life as depicted in this story actually happened.

CHAPTER 1 ∾

ON CLEAR DAYS the stretch of ocean separating Plum Cove Island from the coast of Maine is green and glistens like my cousin Caleb's eyes. But on that half-lit morning of Caleb's arrival, the deep water was as murky as the tide flat. Everything about that day, June 25, 1970, was gray — gray water, gray sky, and the gray ferry appearing like a ghost from the fog. It was one of those days when color is absent and only values of light and dark define the landscape.

Chiaroscuro is my favorite word. It means shadings of light and dark in a work of art without regard to color. I love the sound of it. Key-are-o-scooro. It rolls off my tongue. I like to dream that someday I'll be known as Molly Todd, the famous chiaroscurist. Not a painter like my Uncle John, who worked in color, but an illustrator whose tools are pencil and charcoal, pen and ink.

As I waited on the dock for the ferry, the gray landscape appeared in sharp contrast to our last summer on the island nine years earlier. That summer, when Caleb was twelve and I barely eight, one cloudless day had followed another with colors as intense as the bright globs of paint on Uncle John's palette. Uncle John once told me that when Caleb was a baby he had stared at the ocean so long his blue eyes changed to green, and I had believed him. No one else in our family has green eyes.

That summer was the last time I had seen Caleb. Now, nine years later, after being wounded in Vietnam and discharged with a Silver Star and Purple Heart, he was coming home to the island to heal. I had been sent to fetch him.

Peering through the mist at the ferry crossing the three-mile stretch from the town of New Dover on the mainland, I felt uneasy, as though waiting to meet some stranger. I wiped my sweaty palms down the legs of my blue jeans and watched the boat approach with feelings of dread and anticipation churning my stomach. What does a girl just turned seventeen, for whom life has been easy, say to a man of twenty-one who has just returned from a war in which he had almost lost his life?

I needn't have worried. From the moment he stepped off the ferry and greeted me, it was clear Caleb McLaughlin was not interested in a lot of casual conversation. I also needn't have worried about not recognizing him. Only a half dozen people were on the ferry when it docked, and only one was a young man who walked with a pronounced limp and carried a cane.

I would have known him anyway. Before he spotted me, I had the advantage of being able to watch him from a distance. He was wearing blue jeans, combat boots, and an army fatigue jacket with unfaded patches of cloth that revealed all the usual patches and insignia had been cut off. He stood outlined against the dark water, one narrow hip thrust forward, head tilted to the side. He had the same straight, almost aquiline nose and high cheekbones as Uncle

John, and the same deep russet shock of hair that fell across his forehead.

What struck me most of all, though, was his expression. As a child, I remembered him always grinning, looking as though he either were planning mischief or had just finished doing it. Now not even the hint of a smile lightened the brooding look that shadowed his face. Even though his skin had the pallor of someone who has been ill a long time, I would have shaded his face in darkness if I had sketched him at that moment.

He looked up, caught me staring, and frowned. I felt a moment of panic as I suddenly wondered if he would expect me to kiss him or shake his hand, but I was spared the embarrassment of making the wrong decision by the fact that I could do neither. One of his hands was encumbered by the cane, and the other clutched a large duffel bag swung over his shoulder. A guitar hung by a strap across his chest. So I stuffed my hands into my jeans pockets and shook back my waist-length dark hair. Taking a deep breath, I stepped forward to claim him.

"You must be Caleb," I said with a nervous attempt at a smile. "I'm . . . "

"Molly," he said, finishing my sentence. "I haven't forgotten you, Molly," he continued as his eyes flickered over me. "You used to hide under my bed and spy on me."

I looked at his face to see if he was joking, and that was when I noticed his eyes were still green.

"Don't worry," I said. "I don't do that anymore. And I only did it to get even with you for dangling jellyfish in my face."

"I guess we've both grown up some since then." For the first time the hint of a smile lightened his face.

Leaning his cane against his right leg, he held out his hand for me to shake. Even on such a damp and chilly June day, his palm was warm, the skin somewhat rough, like the surface of a cat's tongue. Although the skin on his hand and lower arm was very pale and strangely mottled, the handshake was firm and muscular. Aunt Phoebe had told us about his right leg being shattered when a land mine exploded in front of him, but she hadn't said anything about burns or skin grafts on his arm.

I felt at a loss for something else to say. I, whom my father had nicknamed Blabby when I was a child, was suddenly tongue-tied.

"Don't ask Caleb about Vietnam," Mother had warned me and my little brother, P.J., on more than one occasion. "He's coming here to recuperate and forget about the war, not answer a lot of questions about it." But I couldn't think of any topic to talk about except the war.

"He'll want to go off by himself," Aunt Phoebe had written in a letter shortly before Caleb's arrival. "He spends too much time alone. Even when he's with other people he tends to disappear inside himself. He calls it thinking, but I call it brooding. In many ways he reminds me of his father."

I was suddenly faced with the knowledge that I was the one who would have to spend the most time with him. A good part of every day, Mother was holed up preparing a brief for some complicated law case. And at ten, P.J. was too young to be of much interest to someone like Caleb. So that left me to fill the gap. I was not to ask him about the war, he was not to be left alone, and already I was struggling for something to talk about. The summer loomed ominously.

"Let me take something," I said for the lack of anything better to say. "I can carry your duffel."

He unslung his guitar. "Take this," he said and held it out to me. "It makes it hard to walk, and I'm slow enough without it."

He limped toward the cars parked at the end of the pier. Careful to match my pace to his, I fell into step beside him. I rummaged wildly for a topic of conversation, but Caleb seemed unaware of my nervousness. His restless eyes shifted from the tall-masted sloops moored in the harbor to the seagulls perched on weathered pilings along the shore.

At the end of the pier he paused to look up the main street that wound through town, its houses running in a scraggly line behind the sidewalks. "It hasn't changed much, has it?" he said flatly.

"You probably remember it a lot better than I do," I said, relieved to find a safe topic. "Here in Bucks Harbor things look pretty much the same. But across the island, around Windhover, there's been a lot of new construction. New summer houses mostly, like the one we bought, and some new stores. You know, touristy things like tearooms and needlepoint shops."

I fell silent, remembering that my family fit this category — tourists, summer people — whereas Caleb had lived on the island for almost thirteen years. I wondered what it was like to come back after so many years away and what he must be feeling after all that had happened in the nine years since his family had left Plum Cove. I felt embarrassed that we could afford to buy a summer home on the island when they had been forced to leave their home and move to St. Louis.

I glanced at him sideways, fearful my face revealed my thoughts, but he seemed lost in his own thoughts.

"It's the blue Jeep," I said, pointing. He threw his duffel in the open rear end, while I laid the guitar on the back seat. With some awkwardness he climbed into the high passenger seat beside me and stretched out his right leg stiffly in front of him. I wanted to ask him if it was still painful but thought maybe that fell under the category of war topics, so I stayed silent.

Even in late June, the town of Bucks Harbor was almost empty, the main street still unclogged by the streams of cars that would bring trafffic to a standstill by the middle of August. As we drove along the nearly deserted main street, the bells of Plum Cove's Episcopal church chimed noon. As though in response to the bells, the haze began to thin, revealing the pale sun directly overhead. Here on the harbor side of the island facing the mainland, the fog was rising, but near Windhover, on the ocean side, the mist would still be hugging the ground.

In the chilly, damp air, Caleb looked out the open window beside him and raised his face to the colorless circle of light as though seeking warmth. But his expression still had that dark look that made him seem to be hiding some secret.

I concentrated on the road and tried to suppress a shiver. "Would you like to drive around the island?" I asked. "Or would you rather go straight to the house?"

"Let's take the shore road," he replied without hesitation. "Unless Aunt Libby's expecting us for lunch at a certain time."

"Mother's probably buried in her brief," I said. "Until this trial is over, the hour we eat is the least of her concerns."

"Sounds important," Caleb said without turning from the window.

"I really don't know much about it except that it's some big government antitrust case and the company is freaking out. When Mother's not buried in stacks of legal papers, she's on the phone to New York. But she'd still much rather work here than in the city."

"You were here last summer, too, weren't you?"

"Yes, but we just rented a house then. Mother wanted to be sure both P.J. and I liked it on Plum Cove before buying anything. The last time we were here, P.J. was only a year old, and of course he didn't remember the island at all."

"I'm not sure I'd even recognize P.J.," Caleb said.

"Well, I guess not!" I replied with a laugh. "He doesn't look like a baby anymore, that's for sure. For a ten-year-old, he's not so bad," I added, wanting to give P.J. a good advance notice.

It crossed my mind that last summer, while Mother, P.J., and I were testing the island in our rented house, Caleb was fighting somewhere in the jungles of Vietnam. He hadn't been drafted. He had enlisted, although I often wondered why. The image of a mountain of the black body bags used to carry dead soldiers flickered through my mind. For a moment I had the strange sensation that one of them was Caleb, and the shiver I had tried to suppress ran down my spine.

"Where exactly is it?" Caleb asked.

"Where's what?" I asked, feeling foolish at not following the conversation.

"Your house."

I squirmed uncomfortably. "Actually, it's at the other end

of the cove from your old house. Almost directly across the harbor from it, about a half mile up from the village. On clear days we can see your house across the cove. It's for sale, so it's empty now."

I didn't add that Mother had seriously considered buying it but decided the old place held too many memories. Since Uncle John's death and my parents' divorce seven years ago, Mother has tried to view everything as a fresh start, a new beginning, and her brother's house held too much of the past, too many memories of those happier years before their lives began to fall apart.

"Would you like to see your house again?" I asked, turning to face Caleb. "We could drive by it before going home."

"No," Caleb said sharply, his face tightening, and I was sorry I had made the suggestion. "I'd like to see it once before it's sold," he added after a moment, "but not today."

He swung his face away, and I wondered if he, too, was remembering those more carefree years on the island.

We started around the long curve that sweeps across the south end of the island to the eastern shore. On this side of the island, the pale sphere of the sun had disappeared again behind fog that drifted through the open windows of the Jeep. I turned on the headlights and slowed down.

We headed up the road that climbs to the peak of the bluff, then winds down again past our house into the village of Windhover and up to Caleb's old house on the other side of the cove. As we neared the bluff, the pine trees thinned and the distance between the houses increased. Not everyone wanted to live on the high ground where in winter the wind swept out of the northeast and howled across the rocky bluff.

We rounded the curve and came to the highest point on

the island, marked by an old, abandoned lighthouse.

"Stop here for a minute," Caleb commanded.

Startled, I pulled off the road into the grass that ran beside the shoulder. Before the Jeep had come to a full stop, Caleb had his door open and climbed out, limping across the grass in long, awkward strides.

He walked to the edge of the bluff overhanging the open sea and stood so close to the edge that one accidental misstep — or a deliberate one — could have sent him over the edge. I hurried to him. He glanced at me, but we stood without speaking, looking out across the water where a stubborn layer of fog still drifted.

High Point divided the open sea from the cove, and from where we stood we could see the two faces of the ocean. On one side the waves broke against the rocks with the whole force of the Atlantic Ocean. On the other side the waters lay more quietly. The cove gathered the white water and cradled it after it had spent its fury.

On the far side of the cove, a single schooner was moored. Barely visible through the mist, it had a ghostly look, as though it were built of air and water and might at any moment disappear.

"Look," I said, pointing in the direction of the schooner. "It looks just like the ship in 'The Rime of the Ancient Mariner.'"

"You know that poem?" Caleb asked with a look of surprise. "I didn't think anybody read it anymore."

"We had to read it for English class last year. Mr. Daniels makes all his English classes read it. It's one of his favorite poems."

It was also one of my favorites. In art class I drew an illustration of the mariner with the albatross hanging around his neck, staring with glittering eyes at the spectres that had once been the shipmates. Very moody. I gave the drawing to Mr. Daniels, who actually had it framed and hung it above the blackboard at the front of his classroom.

Caleb turned and walked around the edge of the bluff that ran down to the cove. Halfway down was our house, but today it wasn't visible from where we stood. I let him go and watched the ship across the cove. The wind was rising, and I lifted my face to it, knowing it would blow the fog out to sea.

I knew Mother would probably have lunch ready by now. I started toward Caleb to tell him we should go, but stopped. He was staring at something below him in the cove. From where I stood at the top of the bluff, I couldn't see what he was looking at, but again he was leaning so far out over the edge that I was alarmed. I followed him, but this time the thought struck me that if he fell he could take me with him, and I kept some distance between us. I was sorry Mother had sent me to get him in the first place, and especially sorry I had ever stopped the Jeep.

Caleb paid no attention to me but continued to stare down at the cove. His face, paler than when I had first seen him on the dock, was as still as if it had been carved from stone. It reminded me of one of the spectres on the mariner's ship.

I looked down, following the direction of his eyes. For a moment I couldn't see anything out of the ordinary, just the mist and rocks and rolling surf. But then through the fog a figure emerged, the vague form of what seemed to be a young girl with long, pale blond hair blowing in the wind.

The girl stood looking out to sea, her legs firmly planted on the outgrowth of rock. Her dress, colorless in the gray light, hung almost to her ankles. She wore an old-fashioned cap, the kind that seemed to be tied under her chin. Although I couldn't see her feet clearly, I sensed they were bare. But even as I strained to see, the mist swirled in front of me, blurring my vision and making the girl appear without form, almost surreal. As though sensing our presence, she turned and raised her head to face us.

In the fog, she couldn't possibly have seen more than two vague shapes above her on the bluff, but I had the distinct impression, a sudden feeling, that she was staring directly into Caleb's eyes. The back of my neck and scalp prickled.

I was about to ask Caleb if he, too, had the feeling she was looking right at him, but the look on his face halted my words. It was a look I could have captured on paper but find hard to describe in words, the look of someone tormented. I reached out to touch him, but he drew away and I pulled back my hand.

"What a strange-looking girl," I said at last. "Where do you suppose she's from?"

For a moment I thought he wasn't going to answer, but then he spoke in a low voice.

"It wasn't a girl."

"Not a girl?" I repeated.

"No," he said. "When I first looked down and saw her, she was bent over, stooped. She was an old lady with long white hair blowing in the wind."

"Oh, it must have been the fog!" I said quickly and wondered if Caleb's experiences in Vietnam had affected his mind as well as his body. The thought made me shiver, and I looked again to reassure myself that it really was a young girl I had seen.

But when I looked, the girl was gone, disappeared, as though she had been swallowed suddenly by the sea.

CHAPTER 2 ∾

I WAS GRATEFUL we were less than a mile from home. On the short drive to our house, neither Caleb nor I mentioned the girl on the rocks, but all my earlier misgivings about the summer seemed like a premonition come true.

Although I had questioned Caleb's state of mind, I found it hard to believe he might really be having delusions. I knew, though, that fog could play strange tricks on the imagination, make someone think he sees something that's not really there. But Caleb was well acquainted with fog, and he had sounded so certain about the old woman changing into a young girl. The only other explanation, that the figure was some strange apparition, made me shake my head in disbelief.

I glanced at Caleb and saw his face was the color of ashes.

"There it is," I said to divert him and pointed down the hill to our house just coming into view through the mist. I turned into the dirt drive, stopping for a moment near the road. "From here we can see your house when it's clear."

Caleb leaned out the window, straining to see. Although by now the houses and shops of Windhover were visible, up the hill beyond the town everything was still wrapped in a shroud of fog. I pulled up the drive and parked beside the house, honking twice to let Mother know we had arrived.

I could see P.J. in the front hall, standing with his face pressed against one of the glass panels flanking the door. He was waiting for Mother before coming out to greet Caleb, the cousin he couldn't remember.

"Hey, P.J., we're here!" I called, and the front door slowly opened. Mother appeared behind him and passed him on the veranda, reaching Caleb well ahead of P.J., who hung back on the steps. As Mother opened her arms to embrace Caleb, I was aware of how alike they were with their auburn hair, fair skin, and the McLaughlin nose. With our dark hair and eyes, P.J. and I resembled the Todd side of the family.

Mother kissed Caleb on both cheeks, and he smiled in return, the first real smile I had seen. I was almost sorry I hadn't kissed him myself on the dock.

"Caleb. It's good to see you," Mother said, holding him at arm's length to get a good look at him. "We're so glad you're here. Stay as long as you want. The whole summer."

Mother always spoke in short, simple sentences, a habit she had acquired after six years of examining witnesses and addressing juries.

"I might take you up on that, Aunt Libby," Caleb said. "You don't know how happy I am to be here. It's been a long time." He turned and looked out at the ocean.

"Too long," Mother said firmly. The last time she had seen Caleb was at Uncle John's funeral seven years ago, and I knew she couldn't help but notice how much Caleb looked like Uncle John. I wondered if the daily reminder would bother her.

With one arm around Caleb's waist, she started toward

the house but stopped again as P.J. came down the stairs one at a time, dragging his feet on each step. "Caleb, this is Peter John. Better known as P.J.," she said. "The last time you saw him, he wasn't even walking."

"No, but he sure could get around on those hands and knees." Although Caleb spoke without a smile, his face seemed softer, the muscles in his cheeks less tense. "I'll bet you've still got the calluses to prove it, P.J."

"Naw," P.J. replied with an embarrassed blush, nudging back the glasses that had, as usual, slipped to the end of his nose. "I do better now on two feet."

"Lunch is ready whenever you are," Mother said, continuing up the steps to the front door. "I put you on the third floor, Caleb. It's the most private. I hope all the stairs won't be a problem. If they are, you can trade rooms with P.J."

"They won't be a problem," Caleb said. "I'm supposed to exercise my leg all I can."

The two of them disappeared inside, leaving P.J. and me to carry in the duffel and guitar.

"Here, Twerp," I said, handing him the guitar, "but be careful. Don't drop it."

"Wow, this is really cool," he said, rubbing his fingers over the polished wood. "Maybe he'll teach me to play it."

"Maybe. But don't bug him about it."

"Of course not," he said heading for the house with a look of reproach in my direction. "I'm not ignorant."

Holding the guitar firmly in both hands, he nudged open the door with his knee and scooted inside. Before it closed, I heard him call, "Hey, Caleb, will you show me how to play the guitar?"

I hauled the duffel out of the rear of the Jeep. Leaving it on the grass, I walked down the drive to the edge of the bluff. Looking back, I tried to see the house as though for the first time, as Caleb had seen it. It still had the raw look of new cedar shake siding, but by next summer the salt spray would have weathered it to a soft dove gray. Across the front of the house and along one side stretched the wide veranda.

I loved the house, but it was the property that had sold Mother on buying it. The house came with two acres. The front acre was a grassy knoll that appeared as an unexpected rise halfway down the road to Windhover. The house sat on the rise, putting it in the path of the summer breezes and providing a view of the town and both sides of the rocky cove that curved like a half-moon from point to point.

The back acre sloped down to a wooded thicket of white pines and beech trees, one of the few wooded areas on the island's coast. Over the years, the rise must have protected the trees from the salt spray and icy winter winds. Hidden from the main house, an old log hut squatted in the center of the thicket, a ramshackle relic from some earlier time, judging from its condition. I hoped to convert it into a studio.

But the best part of the property was the fact that below where I was standing, down the rocky slope that stretched into the water, lay a small strip of sand, the only beach along the southern arm of the cove. Clambering over the wet rocks after high tide could be tricky, but having our own private beach made it worth the slippery climb down to it. I only hoped that Caleb would be able to maneuver the rocks with his lame leg. As soon as the weather warmed, I planned to spend a lot of time stretched out on that strip of sand.

I looked down at the spot where we had seen the girl in the fog. She had been standing on the rocks, not more than a few yards from the sand beach, and I realized now that she had been almost directly below our house. I scanned the whole length of the cove but saw no one and no sign that anyone had been there.

By the time I got the duffel inside the house, Mother and P.J. were having lunch in the kitchen.

"Where's Caleb?" I asked.

"He went to lie down for a while," she said, cutting an orange into eight equal wedges. "He took his sandwich upstairs with him. It's just as well. I think he was pretty worn out. He had to catch the bus at the crack of dawn to get to New Dover in time for the noon ferry." P.J. reached for a piece of orange and sucked on it noisily. Mother frowned but otherwise ignored him. "I imagine coming back to the island was wearing in itself. I hope you didn't talk his arm off."

"As a matter of fact," I said testily, "he didn't have much to say, so I didn't either."

P.J. looked up from his orange wedge, glancing from Mother to me with a worried frown. He hated it when we argued — a holdover, I think, from the quarrels Mother and Daddy used to have, which must have been some of P.J.'s earliest memories.

Once I overheard Mother tell a friend of hers that she got pregnant with P.J. to try and keep her marriage together but that a new baby had only made matters worse. I never breathed a word of this to P.J., of course, but I often wondered if he somehow sensed it. It didn't help that he looked just like our father, with his dark skin, wide-set eyes, and long lashes, lashes any girl would kill for.

I wished Mother would pay more attention to P.J., but every time I mentioned it she said he was fine and could fight his own battles without my help. I wasn't so sure. But now, for his sake, I just shrugged my shoulders and sat down to eat my sandwich.

"So did Caleb say he'd teach you to play the guitar?" I asked P.J.

His face brightened. "Yeah, he said we could begin tonight, right after supper."

"Great."

I watched P.J. spear a dill pickle out of the jar with a fork and take a large bite. The thought of dill pickle on top of orange made me shiver, but I didn't say anything, not even when juice ran down his chin into his collar. I was glad Caleb would be spending time with him and was only a little envious that it would be P.J. rather than I who would be learning to play the guitar.

"How does he seem to you?" Mother asked. "You know. In general."

"Okay," I answered slowly, not sure exactly what I did think. "A bit strange, maybe."

"Strange? In what way?"

I was going to mention the girl on the rocks that Caleb had thought was an old lady, but by then somehow it seemed less important and not so strange, considering the fog.

"Oh, mostly just kind of quiet," I said instead. "You know, like he thinks a lot."

"Well, that's not so surprising, considering all he's been through." Mother rose and carried her plate to the sink. "I've got some work to finish. But let me know when he wakes up. I have lobsters for supper. If the weather clears, we can cook them on the beach." She paused, a frown puckering the space between her eyes. "Or perhaps not," she said vaguely and left the kitchen.

"What's the matter with her?" P.J. said.

"Oh, Uncle John had his own lobster traps, and we used to steam lobsters and clams down on the beach when he was alive," I explained, remembering the evenings we had gathered on the beach at sundown.

"Heck," P.J. said, getting up from the table and heading out of the kitchen, "I don't think lobster's so great. And clams are gross."

I let him go without even reminding him to stack his dirty plate and glass in the dishwasher. I felt sad that P.J. didn't have any memories of those good times. Ever since Uncle John's death, Mother backed away from any reminder of him. I didn't know if it was because she was still grieving for him or because she had never been able to forgive him for killing himself.

Two years after Uncle John left the island with his family, he committed suicide in his garage in St. Louis. He turned on the car's engine one day and waited to die. That night, when Aunt Phoebe called to break the news to us, was probably the worst night of my life, and it's still hard for me to think about it. Luckily, P.J. had already been put to bed, but I was in the kitchen with Mother.

It was Daddy who answered the phone, and I've often wondered if things might have turned out differently if it had been Mother who took the call and heard the news direct from Aunt Phoebe instead of my father. As it was, Daddy broke the news to us together. Mother's face grew as still as chiseled marble, and she didn't utter a sound. I still remember how Daddy went to her, tried to put his arms around her, but she turned away from him. She went into their bedroom and closed the door.

When I saw the look of hurt on Daddy's face, I began to

cry in great gulping sobs, and I wept for Uncle John and my father together. Daddy took me in his arms and held me until, a long time later, my tears finally stopped and he wiped my face with his handkerchief.

Uncle John killed himself just six months before Mother and Daddy separated. I always connected the two events in my mind, and I still wonder if Uncle John's death had anything to do with the divorce. Mother never talked about either one, and I wasn't surprised when she decided against buying Uncle John's house.

With a heavy feeling in my stomach, I cleared away P.J.'s and my lunch dishes. If P.J. had no happy memories of summers on the island, he at least had no painful memories of the night Aunt Phoebe called. For that I was thankful.

*

That night after supper I put on a jacket and went outside to sit alone on the veranda. Even though the fog had finally lifted, the evening had been too cool for a cookout on the beach, and we ended up eating our lobsters at the kitchen table. After supper Mother had disappeared upstairs, and P.J. headed to the living room with Caleb for his first guitar lesson.

Out on the porch, I chose a rocker near the front window, turning it to face inside so that I could watch Caleb and P.J. and hear the lesson through the partially opened window.

They were sitting side by side on the sofa, P.J.'s dark head bent beneath Caleb's lighter one. In the lamplight Caleb's hair gleamed red-gold. He placed the guitar across P.J.'s left knee and wrapped the fingers of his left hand around the neck, leaving P.J.'s right hand free to strum the strings.

"This is the neck of the guitar, and these are the frets," Caleb explained, pointing to the narrow ridges along the neck. He named the six strings and demonstrated how different notes were played as he plucked each string and pressed each fret along the neck.

"Chords are formed by holding down several strings at the same time. The trick is moving your fingers easily from one to another. While the left hand plays chords, the right hand plays the melody. It's a little bit like patting your head and rubbing your tummy," he said, and P.J. looked up at him with a smile. "This is the A chord," Caleb continued, placing P.J.'s fingers on the neck of the guitar.

He showed P.J. how to run the pick across the strings, and a chord sounded. P.J. glanced up again with a pleased look, as though surprised he had been the one to make the sound. For the next half hour Caleb took P.J. through the beginning steps, showing him the basic chords and how to move his fingers, over and over until P.J. could play the chords in succession.

I could see the two of them in the lighted room through the window and at the same time see my own reflection in the glass. Although my hair and eyes were darker than P.J.'s and my father's, almost black like Aunt Phoebe's, I was surprised to see that in certain features Caleb and I looked alike. We had the same broad forehead and high cheekbones, the same mouth with the fuller lower lip and upper lip that curved upward like a bow.

I was startled by the similarities until I remembered we weren't just cousins but double first cousins, making the blood ties between Caleb and me very close. Not only had Uncle John been Mother's brother, but also Aunt Phoebe was my father's sister. He and Mother had met at Uncle John and Aunt Phoebe's wedding and married the following year.

Caleb seemed less strained and more at ease with P.J. this evening than he had with me earlier in the day. I wondered if it was P.J. who made the difference or simply the fact that I was seeing Caleb from a distance.

"You're a natural," Caleb said to P.J. "You'll be playing all the coffeehouses in no time."

"Thanks," P.J. said, squirming as he always did when he was embarrassed. "And thanks a lot for the lesson."

"That's probably enough for one night. One step at a time."

"You play something," P.J. said, holding the guitar out to Caleb. "Please."

Caleb took the guitar and hung the strap across his shoulder, cradling it against his chest. He ran his fingers across the strings and played a few chords in quick succession, pausing a moment to tighten one of the strings. I could tell right away he was good, but I didn't know how good until he started to play.

He began softly, moving his fingers from one fret to another faster than my eye could follow, playing chords much more complex than those he had taught P.J., as well as a melody. He played some song that sounded classical, something I didn't recognize. Then his hands slowed, the music grew quieter as he shifted into a different song.

After the first few bars, I recognized "Blowin' in the Wind" by Bob Dylan. Halfway through the first verse, he began to sing the lyric, softly at first but gradually louder, and something about the way he sang made me pay special attention to the words.

> *Yes, 'n' how many seas must a white dove sail*
> *Before she sleeps in the sand?*

Yes, 'n' how many times must the cannonballs fly
Before they're forever banned?
The answer, my friend, is blowin' in the wind,
The answer is blowin' in the wind.

A shiver ran down my spine. His voice rose full and rich in the night, a counterpoint to the sound of the waves breaking on the rocks at high tide. P.J. was hunched back into the corner of the sofa, watching Caleb with wide eyes.

As Caleb moved into the second verse, I leaned into the patch of light from the window to hear more clearly.

How many years can a mountain exist
Before it's washed to the sea?
Yes, 'n' how many years can some people exist
Before they're allowed to be free?
Yes, 'n' how many times can a man turn his head,
Pretending he just doesn't see?
The answer, my friend, is blowin' in the wind,
The answer is blowin' in the wind.

When Caleb came to the lines about a man turning his head and pretending not to see, his eyes closed. His voice softened again. He seemed to be singing for himself and had forgotten P.J. In the lamplight Caleb's face appeared older than his twenty-one years. He looked like a man remembering things he wanted to forget.

Moving forward in the rocker, I watched his face and listened as he sang the last verse.

How many times must a man look up
Before he can see the sky?
Yes, 'n' how many ears must one man have
Before he can hear people cry?

Yes, 'n' how many deaths will it take till he knows
That too many people have died?
The answer, my friend, is blowin' in the wind,
The answer is blowin' in the wind.

He hummed the chorus again softly, and his fingers came to rest on the strings. In the light, the polished wood of the guitar gleamed.

I sat without moving, hoping he would begin another song, but he unslung his guitar and stood up.

P.J. looked up at him from the other end of the sofa. "Gee, you're really good, Caleb," he said. "You ought to make records."

For a moment Caleb looked off into space as though returning from some great distance. Then he turned to P.J. "I hope some record company agrees with you," he said with a brusque laugh. "But you've got talent yourself, P.J. Let me know when you want another lesson."

P.J. glowed. "Sure, Caleb, any time you say."

Caleb yawned and stretched. "Right now I think I'll call it a day."

P.J. followed Caleb out of the room and up the stairs. I could hardly believe he was voluntarily going to bed. Usually P.J. could always find one more thing to do at bedtime. Neither of them even glanced in my direction on the veranda, and I felt somehow invisible and thus forgotten.

With a sigh I went into the house and searched for the mystery I was reading. I could hear Mother banging away on her typewriter in her bedroom and knew she was probably set for the night.

I turned out all the lights except one in the hallway, but I didn't bother to lock the doors. Nobody ever locked doors

on Plum Cove Island. After all, where was a thief or mur-
derer to go?

Up in my bedroom I settled into bed with my mystery,
but I had a hard time keeping my mind on the story. The
girl on the beach was a greater mystery. I wondered who
she was and where she had come from.

I must have dozed, because the next thing I knew I was
still sitting up in bed with the light on, my book in my lap.
But the clock on my bedside table read almost midnight,
and I reached over to turn out the light. I had just snuggled
under the covers when I heard the door of the attic room
above me open, and seconds later muffled footsteps sounded
on the stairs as though someone were trying to walk as
quietly as possible. I listened as the footsteps passed my
door and continued down to the first floor. The front door
opened and closed.

I climbed out of bed and went to the window, crouching
so that only my eyes would be visible above the windowsill.
On my knees I watched Caleb limp down the stretch of
rough grass in front of the house and cross the road to where
the rocky coast descended in a steep incline to the ocean.
Through the open window I heard distant waves breaking
on the rocks beyond the cove, the spray tossed high in a
silvery cloud. Except for a bank of scudding clouds, the sky
was brilliant with stars, the moon almost full. Only an occasional cloud darkening the moon shadowed the night.

Caleb climbed slowly across the face of the rocks, teetering
once or twice and then bending to steady himself with one
hand. The image of a body lying broken on the rocks crept
into my mind. My first thought was that I should follow
and try to stop him, but the memory of standing beside him
at the very edge of the cliff swept over me, and I inched

away from the window. For the second time that day I let Caleb go on by himself.

Just as I was about to start back to bed, there was a lull in the crash of the waves. In the sudden stillness I heard the sound of someone moaning, a low keening like someone grieving. I held my breath and listened. The sound of the cries faded, and I wondered if it could have been some animal that sounded strangely human. I scanned the stretch of moonlit road and grass beside it but saw nothing.

Then the mournful sound began again, and it was clearly the cry of a woman. The hairs rose on the back of my neck. Straining to see in the moonlight, I peered out, waiting, but no one came into view, and in the night it was impossible to determine the direction of the cries. I thought again of the girl on the beach, wondering who and where she was.

The waves surged once more, drowning out the sound of the crying. By the time they washed out again, it had stopped. Except for the sound of water sluicing across the rocks, the night was silent. I crept back to bed, worried about Caleb and disturbed by a cry of such despair. I wondered if Caleb had heard it, too.

I lay awake, stiff under the taut sheet and blanket pulled up to my chin. At last I heard Caleb return and climb the stairs again to his room. Knowing he was safely home, I could at last fall into a troubled sleep.

CHAPTER 3 ∽

I SLEPT LATE the following morning. By the time I got to the kitchen for breakfast, neither Caleb nor P.J. was in sight. Only Mother was still at the table, allowing herself the luxury of an extra cup of coffee and a cigarette.

Making loud gagging and coughing noises, I waved at the smoke.

"I get your message, Molly," Mother said. "No need to knock yourself out." Taking a last drag, she stubbed the end of her cigarette into the ashtray.

"Is Caleb still sleeping?" I asked.

"No. He finished breakfast an hour ago and went down to the beach. P.J. went with him."

"The public beach or ours?"

"Ours."

I poured a glass of orange juice, then reached for a bowl and filled it half full of cornflakes. I added some milk and sat down at the table opposite her. I knew I should mention something about Caleb's solitary midnight wanderings along the shore. But now, in the light of day, my fears about going after him struck me as cowardice, and I was too ashamed to bring it up.

"Did you hear anything strange last night?" I asked after a moment, trying to keep my voice casual. The memory of that sad, moaning cry haunted me even in the daylight.

"Hear anything?" Mother repeated. "No. Not a thing. I slept soundly all night. Why?"

"I thought I heard someone crying outside," I said, "but I didn't see anyone. I couldn't tell exactly where it was coming from."

"Probably some animal. Or maybe the ocean. It can sound strange sometimes."

"Maybe," I agreed.

Mother nursed the last few sips of her coffee, then pushed back her chair and stood up. "Time to get to work," she said with a sigh.

"Why don't you take the morning off and come down to the beach with us?" I asked. "Or just goof off for a change?"

For a second I thought she might take me up on it, but then she shook her head and started for the door.

"Can't," she said. "I'd like to. I really would. But this has to get done. The trial's coming up in six weeks. Maybe when all the preparation for it's over I can begin to enjoy being here. But right now . . . " Her voice trailed off as she disappeared through the door.

I finished breakfast alone, quickly loaded the dirty dishes into the dishwasher, and stepped outside on the veranda. After yesterday's fog the day had dawned bright and clear without even a hint of haze to dull the blue of the sky or the green of the pine trees that glimmered in the sun. It was the kind of day that almost made me change my mind about being an artist who doesn't work with color.

Grabbing my sketch pad and box of charcoal and pencils, I followed the path Caleb had taken last night. I was dressed only in sneakers and a T-shirt and shorts, but today the sun warmed even the breeze off the ocean. The tide was out, the water quiet. Peering in the direction of the sand beach, I spotted the two of them.

Caleb was stretched face up on the sand. A few yards away P.J. was standing on a rock at the edge of the water, feeding bread to the gulls wheeling above him. P.J. always made a point of feeding only the gulls who dared to snatch the bread from his upraised fingers, whereas I always chickened out and dropped the piece of bread at the last second. As soon as P.J. ran out of bread, the gulls flew off over the water in search of another meal.

P.J. moved along the face of the rock, squatting now and then in search of starfish or other treasures of the ocean in the pools of water that collected in the crevices of the rocks. I climbed down the rocks to the edge of the sand where Caleb was lying, but he seemed unaware of my approach. His eyes were closed.

Beside him lay an open tube of suntan cream. Although it was still only midmorning, I hoped he had used it liberally. In the glare of the sun, his skin had that pallor that comes from being in a hospital too long. Although his shoulders and chest were unmarked and smooth except for the thatch of fine auburn hair on his chest, what I saw below his chest made my heart contract. A long, white scar sliced in a narrow arc across his stomach, disappearing beneath the top of his swim trunks.

But what riveted me were his legs. On his left leg, two short scars, white and shiny, marked the upper thigh and a longer one ran down the curve of his calf. His right leg was a mass of scar tissue, purplish and still puckered as though the stitches had only just been taken out. One scar ran all the way from his ankle to the top of his thigh as though the land mine — or perhaps the doctors — had laid open his leg from end to end. Aunt Phoebe had told us he had four operations before they were certain they wouldn't have to amputate. No wonder he had acted yesterday as though there were things he wanted to forget.

Looking at him now lying peacefully on the beach made me ashamed of my earlier doubts and suspicions, and I resolved to make it up to him somehow. I felt an impulse to kneel down and touch the scar on his abdomen, run my finger along the puckered white arc, but I kept my hands at my sides and turned my eyes to P.J. still scavenging on the rocks with a large pail beside him. After last summer P.J. had decided to be a marine biologist.

I looked back at Caleb. His eyes were open, and he was watching me.

"Hi," I said, feeling a bit rattled, thankful he hadn't caught me staring at his legs.

"Hi," was all he said in return.

"I'm sure glad today's better than yesterday."

"So am I," he replied.

I wanted to ask him why he had left the house so late the night before and where he had gone, but he closed his eyes again, and I lost my nerve. He was clearly not in a mood to talk. I sat on a rock at the edge of the strip of sand and opened my sketch pad. The schooner was still anchored across the cove, and I began to draw, trying to capture the feel of the surf and the rolling waves in strokes of black and gray. I worked without pause for a half hour or so, sketching the opposite shore and the Windhover harbor as well as the schooner and the water, then blurring the hard edges and shading the black charcoal into softer grays.

"You're very good," Caleb said over my shoulder, startling me. I hadn't heard him get up. "I mean you're *really* good." He squatted beside me, and I was aware of his shoulder, level with mine, almost touching it.

"Thanks," I mumbled, disconcerted to know he had been watching me.

"Do you paint, too?" he asked me as I continued working with the charcoal.

"Some. But I really like drawing better, or printmaking."

"Do you plan to keep at it?" he asked, looking at me. Today his eyes were a perfect match for the ocean.

"I want to," I said, looking down at my drawing. "Mother wants me to go to Bryn Mawr or Radcliffe after next year, but they're too Ivy League for me. I'd much rather go to an art school. Besides, I've gone to a girls' school all my life. I'd like something different."

"Well, you're good enough for an art school," he said, and I felt as pleased as if some art critic had just awarded me a prize.

"Speaking of being good," I said, flustered and saying the first thing that popped into my head, "I heard you playing last night through the window. I was out on the porch. I hope you don't mind. You're good, too, you know." I paused, thinking that sounded flat. "Not just good, terrific."

"We're a real mutual-admiration society," Caleb said with a sardonic smile, but he stayed where he was beside me. This morning I didn't mind having him there.

"You remind me of Grandpa McLaughlin except that you can sing as well as play," I said. Our grandfather McLaughlin could hear any piece of music once and then sit down at the piano and play it through without a mistake.

But he never had a music lesson because his father thought music was a waste of time. "Do you play by ear, too?" I asked.

"Yes, but I also learned to read music because I wanted to write my own songs."

I looked at him in surprise. Aunt Phoebe had never mentioned that.

"I'd like to hear them sometime." I wasn't just saying that to be polite. I really wanted to hear Caleb sing again and wondered what kind of songs he had written. "Do you write your own lyrics, too?"

"Usually." He picked up an empty clam shell and threw it into the water. "It's funny how genes jump around," he said after a moment. "I inherited the music gene from Grandpa, and you inherited the artistic gene from my father."

"I guess that leaves P.J. to inherit the business gene," I said with a laugh. Grandpa McLaughlin still ran the family business his father had started a hundred years before, the Executive Shoe Company in St. Louis where Uncle John had gone to work after the family moved there.

"He's welcome to it," Caleb said with a vehemence that startled me. He stared out to sea. "If P.J. does go to work there, I hope for his sake it's because he wants to and not because he has to. And if you decide being an artist is what you really want to do, then the most important thing is to stick with it, not give up."

He looked up at the bluff on the far side of the cove, his mouth stiff and unsmiling. Today, in the clear air, his old house was visible on the top of the hill.

"Would you like to go see it today?" I asked with some

misgiving. It didn't take a genius to know this would be one of those times when Aunt Phoebe wouldn't want him to be alone. "We could drive over after lunch if you want."

To my relief he shook his head and turned away. "No," he said, shortly. "Not today, not yet. But I'll tell you what you could do for me."

"What's that?"

"Put some suntan cream on my back." He reached for the tube and squatted beside me, his back turned toward me. I squirted little dabs of the white cream across his back and began to rub it in, moving my fingers in small circles across his neck and shoulders and then slowly down his back. I got to the top of his trunks and paused, my fingertips resting lightly on the small of his back. His skin was warm and smooth, and my own skin tingled in response. Startled, I drew back my hand.

"Thanks," he said and stood up. The backs of his legs were pale but unscarred. He went back to his towel spread on the sand and stretched out, face down.

I hesitated.

"Do you want me to do the backs of your legs?" I finally asked. "They could burn pretty easily."

"That's okay. I did them earlier." His eyes were closed again, and I could watch him openly.

As Caleb lay on his stomach in the sun with his eyes closed, his face was less strained and more youthful-looking than it had seemed the day before. As I watched him, my earlier misgivings began to evaporate and I felt a special kinship, a closeness I had never felt as a child when the four-year difference in our ages seemed like a lifetime. Without a friend of my own to keep me occupied, I had made a nuisance of myself by trailing around behind Caleb like a stray puppy.

Sometimes he teased me or pretended I was a horse and galloped me around using my two braids as reins. But I was happy for the attention, and he was always careful not to get too rough. And when I hid under his bed to spy on him and his friends, he shooed me out with a grin instead of getting angry as he had every right to do.

I thought again about all he had been through — losing his home on the island and two years later losing his father, then enlisting to fight a war no one seemed to approve of and almost getting killed. He had come home to heal, and I would do what I could to help him. It seemed like the least I could do.

I turned back to the schooner riding gracefully on the gentle swells. Under the bright sun it no longer reminded me of the mariner's ghost ship. With a sigh, I gave myself up to my drawing.

CHAPTER 4 〰

B Y THE TIME we headed back to the house a half hour
later, Caleb's white pallor was tinged with a definite
pink, and during lunch I watched the color on his forehead
and nose gradually deepen to red. Being dark, neither P.J.
nor I tended to burn.

As we finished lunch, I asked Caleb if he wanted to go
back to the beach.

"I don't think he needs any more sun today," Mother said
with a laugh.

"I think you're right." Caleb grimaced. "I'm beginning
to feel the effects."

I thought he would probably disappear upstairs again
right after lunch and was surprised when he turned to me.

"Aunt Libby said you want to convert some house into
a studio," he said. "If you want to start on it this afternoon,
I'll give you a hand."

"Sure," I said, pleased at his unexpected offer of help.
"But it's hardly a house, just a one-room log cabin back in
the woods, and pretty rotted at that. I think lately it's been
home to a lot of little animals."

I was happy to know I'd have company. Something about the place gave me the shivers, perhaps because it was so dark and sunless in the thick stand of pine trees.

"How about you, P.J.?" Caleb asked.

"Naw, that's okay," P.J. said quickly, wrinkling up his nose and blinking hard behind his glasses. "That place is creepy. Anyway, I'm going hunting for specimens."

After lunch I gathered what I thought we might need — a bundle of rags and two buckets of water, one soapy, one clear, a hammer and bag of assorted nails, and a broom. Loaded down, Caleb and I walked across the stretch of sea grass that formed the backside of the rise behind the house. The smell of the ocean and salt air gradually faded into the pungent aroma of pine.

We entered the thicket, and the trees closed around us, shutting out the sun. I shivered in the sudden coolness. As I led the way through the trees, the thick carpet of pine needles deadened our footsteps. A few yards into the thicket, a piece of tin flashing around the cabin's chimney suddenly gleamed in a ray of light that had found its way through an opening in trees. A few more steps brought us into a small clearing.

"I'll be damned," Caleb said, giving a soft whistle of surprise as he saw the cabin. "I thought I knew everything and everybody on the island, but I never knew this was here."

"Well, whoever built it must have wanted privacy," I said, setting one of the buckets on what had once been a small stoop but now was just rotting boards. "At first I thought maybe it had been built for a kids' clubhouse. But it's got a stone foundation and a pretty decent fireplace even though the rest of it is kind of thrown together."

Caleb leaned the broom against the door frame and peered into the single window flanking the narrow door.

"I think it's what the realtors call a 'fixer-upper,' " I said with a laugh, "but as you can see, it's pretty much falling down."

The door had no handle. I pushed against it, and it swung open with an angry creak. "Welcome to my studio," I said with irony. Bowing ceremoniously, I let Caleb precede me into the hut.

The only time I had been in the hut was the day P.J. and I had accidentally stumbled on it while exploring the woods. I thought right away of making it into a studio. Although it was really much too dark for the ideal artist's studio, I had been happy to find a place I could call my own. But being there had made both P.J. and me feel strange, as though we were trespassing, so we hadn't stayed long or been back since. I was glad Caleb was with me today.

"We've got some serious work here," he said with a dubious look.

Cobwebs hung from the low ceiling and across the wall, enclosing the corners of the one room and draping the two windows in a thick curtain of gray. Shaking out one of the rags, I took a couple of large swipes across the front window. The room brightened as a single beam of sunlight filtered through the grimy panes of glass. The only other window faced the back of the property.

I pinched my nose to hold back a sneeze as a cloud of dust and cobweb filaments eddied in the air, along with tiny, green translucent wings of long-dead flies. "What really gets me," I said, "is that no one's broken the windows or stolen the furniture. In New York, it would have been totally vandalized about ten minutes after the owner moved out."

Caleb didn't answer but stood looking around at the plain wooden walls and few pieces of furniture that had been abandoned with the house. In the middle of the room stood an old pine drop-leaf table with one leaf missing, the kind of table someone might discard or give to the Salvation Army. Faint streaks of blue on the top revealed it had once been painted. A rickety wooden chair was pulled up to it.

The stone fireplace was set in one of the walls without a window. Against the wall, on one side of the fireplace, a wide bench had been built that might have served as a bunk. On the other side, a crude wooden cupboard filled the remaining space. The only other piece of furniture was a small wooden rocking chair with curved arms and a spindle back, a child's rocker. I sat down in it, barely squeezing between the arms, my knees almost up to my chin. Although the chair creaked ominously under my weight, I leaned back and it rocked smoothly.

As I sat there, an eerie feeling came over me that someone was watching me. I looked up quickly at Caleb, but he was staring out the front window, his head cocked to one side as though listening to some distant sound. I found myself wondering if someone still lived there, but I knew that wasn't possible. Clearly nothing had disturbed the thick layers of dust or piles of mouse droppings for a good many years.

Even so, I couldn't keep from blurting out the question. "Do you think someone's living here?"

"No," Caleb said, looking around again slowly, "no one could be living here now — not for a long time. But it'd be interesting to know who lived here once."

He shifted his weight, turning his face toward the afternoon sun shining obliquely through the glass. One side of his face fell in shadow while the other side was aglow with light.

I caught my breath, wishing I had brought my sketch pad, wanting to capture that moment and draw him as he stood there in that strange room. His face, both washed in light and hidden in darkness, seemed to reflect unseen wounds. The unease I had felt with him the day before began to creep up my spine, and I rose from the rocker. I wondered if my drawing might expose something buried deep within him.

I could only stand and stare until at last Caleb turned.

"We'd better get at it," he said slowly as he took hold of the broom and began to sweep. He started on the walls, whisking the broom across the boards until they were free of tangled gray webs and captive insects. Then he began on the floor. Finally I shook off my apprehension, took the bucket of soapy water and a rag, and began to scrub where he had swept, washing away years of grime.

When we had finished the floor and walls, I started on the back window with a wet rag while Caleb took the hammer and nails to secure some boards that had worked loose on either side of the fireplace. As I washed the window, I was aware of the whang of the hammerhead against the nail but paid little attention until it stopped and Caleb said to me in a low voice, "Molly, come here a minute."

Presuming he needed some help with a board, I dropped my dirty rag in the bucket and turned to him. But he stood a few feet away from the bunk, behind the little rocker, staring at the empty space, the hammer hanging at his side.

"Come over here a minute," he repeated softly. Puzzled, I moved next to him but saw nothing out of the ordinary.

"Now walk toward the bunk — but slowly."

"What is it?" I asked, but he didn't respond.

I took two tentative steps forward. Then I felt it and my heart jumped. It was something I became aware of, like a presence, only not that definite. But whatever was there was something more defined and firmer than the invisible sense of danger. I gulped a sudden inhalation of air as a quick stab of fear jabbed my stomach. I waited but felt nothing more tangible, just an unseen presence, like a displacement of air.

"You feel it, too?" Caleb said behind me, but I didn't turn to look at him. Although nothing touched me, nothing solid, I had the sensation that something was pressing against me, like a wind at my back only less distinct. I took a stiff step forward, then another, until my knees were almost touching the edge of the bunk. Quietly Caleb moved beside me. I reached for his arm and held onto it, aware of the bones of his wrist beneath my fingers.

"What is it?" I whispered.

"I don't know," he said. "There's something in the cabin with us, but I don't know what. I was about to nail that board when I felt it."

He pointed to a wide board above the end of the bunk abutting the fireplace. One end of the board had sprung loose. I knelt on the bunk and hesitantly reached out a hand to push the board back against the narrow strips of vertical wood along the end of the fireplace, hoping I could perhaps shut in whatever it was that was with us.

"No," Caleb said, reaching over my shoulder. "Don't push it in, pull it off."

I dropped my hand, and the end of the board popped loose again. With one good yank Caleb pulled it off, revealing a narrow opening with very shallow shelves like a doll's cupboard. The shelves were all empty. Caleb thrust his hand into the narrow opening, stretching his fingers down beneath the shelves.

"I can feel something," he said after a moment's exploration. Slowly, carefully, an inch at a time, he pulled out his hand. He was holding a small object that he let drop on the bunk.

It was a miniature rag doll, small enough to fit in one hand, the kind a child might have played with a hundred years ago. Although it was dirty and the colors of the cloth had faded to gray, it had been carefully crafted with yarn hair and a long dress. And at one time tiny features, now barely discernible, had been painted on the small face.

Gingerly I picked it up to examine it. "Somebody's doll. Maybe it belonged to whoever lived here."

"More than likely," Caleb agreed. "It must have fallen off the shelf. There might be more down there, but my hand's too big. I could barely reach the doll. You try."

I hesitated, but the prospect of other hidden treasures outweighed my apprehension of whatever was present. I thrust my hand into the opening, worming my fingers down the narrow shaft. At the bottom, one fingertip touched something cold and hard. I wriggled my fingers and felt two small objects. I grasped them in my fingertips and slowly pulled them out, dropping them on the bunk beside the doll. One was an ivory comb with several teeth missing, the other a flint.

Caleb picked up the flint to examine it. "Somebody must have used this to light a fire."

I reached in again, feeling carefully along the bottom. My fingers met something soft but firm. "There's something else," I said, with a surge of excitement as my fingers identified what felt like paper pages and a cloth binding. "Something like a book."

Carefully I worked the object up the side of the cupboard and pulled it over the top. It was a thin, homemade book with rough-cut paper pages covered by a sewn cloth cover. It felt brittle and was layered with dust. I hardly dared open it for fear it might crumble and fall apart.

"See what's inside," Caleb said, impatiently pulling the book from my hands and opening the cover. I strained to see over his shoulder.

The first page had only three lines, written in a round, childlike script so faded I could barely make it out. Caleb held it up to the light, and silently we read together:

This book belongs to
Evaline Cobb Bloodsworth
New Dover, Maine — September 14, 1824

I heard a sudden noise behind me and turned in time to see the front door fly open, thudding against the wall behind it, making me jump. I looked out in surprise, expecting to see the darkness of an approaching storm or wind gusting through the clearing. But the day was bright and still. The treetops stood motionless. Not a breeze stirred.

In front of the fireplace, the little rocker was moving, rocking back and forth, each movement just a little less than the last, as if someone had been sitting there and then stood up.

CHAPTER 5 ∾

O UR HOUSECLEANING CAME to an abrupt end. In a state of mutual shock, Caleb and I silently gathered up our things and started back through the woods. My mind was on what had just happened in the cabin, and from there my thoughts jumped to the girl on the rocks and the crying I had heard the night before.

"Caleb, by any chance did you hear someone crying last night?" I asked, breaking the silence.

He gave me a quizzical look but shook his head.

"No. No one." He made no mention of his night journey across the rocks.

I explained how I had awakened sometime around midnight and described what I had heard. "It sounded like a woman crying. But not just crying. It was as though someone had died and the woman was grieving." I tried to mimic what I'd heard, but my imitation sounded more like an animal in distress. Caleb tried to hide a smile, and even I couldn't help but laugh.

"Mother thought it was probably just some animal. Hearing myself, I guess I'm not so sure now either. But last night I would have sworn it was a woman crying."

"It might have been," Caleb said. "Just because no one else heard it doesn't mean it wasn't real. Especially with all the other things. . . . " His voice trailed off, and we walked again in silence.

"It really is kind of weird, isn't it?" I said at last in a low voice, as if someone were nearby in the woods who might overhear. "I mean, so many strange happenings just since you came. It's almost like something was waiting for your arrival. Does that sound totally stupid?"

"No, it doesn't."

We came out of the woods onto the grass. Caleb kept walking, leaning heavily on his cane. I felt guilty about leading him over rough ground and letting him work so hard.

When we were almost at the house, I asked the other question that had been weighing on my mind. "Should we tell P.J. and Mother about what happened at the cabin? You know . . . about the door and the rocking chair and everything?"

"Let's show them what we found," he said at last. "The doll and the other things. Of course they'll want to read the book, and that's okay. We can all read it together. But maybe that's all we should mention right now. The rest of it would sound pretty strange. I have a hunch Aunt Libby would say it was just the wind."

I nodded in agreement. "Mother would give us that look. And P.J. would probably want to move. After we found the cabin, he didn't much like the idea of it being back there in our woods."

"Did you tell either of them about seeing the girl on the rocks?"

"No, it never seemed like quite the right moment to bring it up."

"Then maybe it's just as well to keep that between us, too."

He looked at me, and I nodded again, happy it all would stay our secret, at least for the moment.

Both P.J. and Mother were in the kitchen when we went in. Mother was just starting supper, and P.J., looking a little sunburned himself, was rinsing his afternoon's collection of "specimens" at the kitchen sink.

Even Mother seemed interested in what we had found, and when I pulled out Evaline Bloodsworth's book, P.J. wanted to read it immediately. I hesitated, and Caleb backed me up.

"How about if we wait 'til after supper, P.J.?" he said. "Then we can all read it together."

"Okay," P.J. agreed, and I realized that already, after only one day, P.J. would agree to whatever Caleb suggested.

While Mother fried chicken, I peeled cold cooked potatoes and hard-boiled eggs. Mother offered Caleb a beer, and he drank it straight from the can while he helped by chopping celery and onions for the potato salad.

It was nice having everyone working together in the kitchen, and even Caleb laughed a little at P.J.'s corny jokes. If we hadn't had the diary to look forward to, I would have felt sorry when supper was over.

As soon as the dishes were cleared, we gathered around the table, and I opened the little book once again to its title page and began to read.

This book belongs to
Evaline Cobb Bloodsworth
New Dover, Maine — September 14, 1824

I paused to glance at the others. Caleb's chair was tipped back, just out of the circle of light around the table, but P.J. was hunched forward, elbows on the table, chin propped in his hands.

I turned the page and moved the book forward a few inches until the light over the table fell directly onto the open page. It was hard reading the faded script and the old-fashioned handwriting with the *s*'s that looked like *f*'s.

"*Today marks the day of my birth,*" I read slowly, stumbling over the first few sentences, "*the beginning of the twelfth year of my life, but I have little to celebrate.*

"*Mr. Gibbons, our schoolmaster, has given me this book so that I may record the events of my days. I will no longer be attending school, and he prays I will not forget the reading and writing I have struggled so hard to learn. He urges me to write in this book and to keep reading my lessons in the Bible. Papa has told me I will be leaving home soon, perhaps leaving even New Dover, so the gift of this book marks more than the day of my birth. It marks both the end of my schooling and the end of my years at home.*

"*I think it must mark as well the end of my life.*

"*Mother tells me I must put myself in God's hands but I cannot help but think God has turned his back on us.*"

I almost said something about how sad it would be to lose your home at the age of twelve but caught myself when I realized the same thing had happened to Caleb. I quickly turned the page and began again.

"*September 20th. It is certain now that I will leave, but where I will go I do not yet know. Being the eldest, I try to put on a good face for my sisters and brothers, but sometimes it is hard not to cry. I pray my sisters will not also be sent away. My brothers will be needed here to help farm.*"

"But why?" P.J. interrupted. "Why would her father send her away?" In the lamplight, the lenses of his glasses magnified his eyes and his look of indignation. P.J. always came to the rescue of any hurt or homeless creature.

I scanned the next few lines. "That part's coming next," I said to reassure him and continued reading more easily now that I was growing accustomed to Evaline's writing.

"*Last spring the church cast out old Mrs. Booker. It was said she consorted with witches and the Devil, and that she was the cause of the hard winter. But now things are worse than ever before.*

"*This year has been the worst anyone can remember. For all of Papa's hard work, we have nothing to show for it. Every month there has been frost, even during the summer. The seed Papa planted last spring froze in the ground, and now we have no crop and no food set by for winter. Already my stomach cramps from never being full. Our animals starve and the cow no longer gives milk. Papa says he will slaughter her for meat, but then the milk will be gone forever.*"

I glanced up from the book. "It's hard to imagine people actually believed in witches only a hundred and fifty years ago," I said.

"And many still do today," Mother said, "But at least that poor Mrs. — what was her name?"

"Mrs. Booker," P.J. prompted.

"Yes, Mrs. Booker. At least she was only cast out. If she had lived a hundred years earlier, she might have been burned at the stake. And the courts not only allowed it but encouraged it." She shook her head in disbelief. "Thank God at least our legal system has become a little more enlightened." She sounded just like Mr. Daniels when we were reading *The Crucible* in school.

"Were there really witches then?" P.J. asked.

"Of course not," I said.

"The so-called witches were really scapegoats, P.J.," Caleb said.

"What's a scapegoat?" P.J. asked, wrinkling his nose to move his glasses upward.

"Originally scapegoats were animals used as sacrifices," Caleb explained. "People believed they could transfer anything evil that had happened onto a lamb or goat. They drove the animal into the wilderness, and the people believed it carried the evil with them. Sometimes they killed the animals instead."

"But what's that got to do with witches?"

"When animals were no longer considered powerful enough for scapegoats, people were used instead. Later, when the Devil was blamed for all the evil in the world, the scapegoats became the witches who were believed to deal with the Devil. Often they were burned."

"Why didn't they just burn the Devil instead of people?" P.J. was clearly indignant.

Caleb smiled. "Well, that would have made a whole lot more sense. But of course they couldn't ever catch the Devil. So they picked on innocent people instead, usually unmarried women who had no standing in the community and couldn't fight back. People justified it by calling the women witches. But the evil was really in themselves — all the sins they had committed that they kept hidden and secret. So things never really got any better."

"You sure know a lot," P.J. said with a look of awe.

Caleb laughed. "Only because I took a course in primitive religions in college."

I had completely forgotten he had gone to college for two years before enlisting.

"Maybe Evaline Bloodsworth was a witch," P.J. said after a moment's silence.

"Don't be silly, P.J.," I said. "Like Caleb just explained, the women weren't *really* witches."

"I know that," P.J. retorted impatiently. "I mean, maybe they *thought* she was a witch and made her a . . . a . . . you know, one of those things Caleb just said."

"A scapegoat," Mother prompted.

"Yeah, a scapegoat," P.J. repeated.

"Maybe she'll tell us if you give her half a chance, P.J.," I said, impatient myself by this time.

"No need to be sarcastic, Molly," Mother said in a mild voice. With a sigh I turned back to Evaline Bloodworth's diary.

"*In July, my best friend Nellie Wilcox was sold at pauper's auction. I cried for a week. She was auctioned to a family in Fayette and has gone there to live. Now I never see her or hear how it goes for her. At that time Papa swore he would never sell one of us at a pauper's auction. He said our belief in God and faith in the commandments would be our salvation, but now I am to be sold at the next auction. I will be sold to the person who bids the least amount of money for me. Then the town of New Dover will pay him that sum for my lodging for a year, and I must work for him for a year for no wages. My sisters cry and cling to me. Sometimes I fear I will faint from despair and wonder what will become of me.*"

"Good God," Mother said softly. "That poor family!"

"How about poor Evaline?" P.J. muttered. "She's the one I feel sorry for."

"Well, of course poor Evaline. Go on, Molly."

"*October 10th. Perhaps God is merciful after all. I am not to be sold at auction! Someone has told Papa about the cotton mills in the town of Lowell in Massachusetts, and I am to go there to work. Lowell is a three-day journey from New Dover. I will work in one of the mills and live there and pay room and board from my wages. Working at a cotton mill will surely be better than the pauper's auction. I have heard that sometimes widowers or unmarried men bid for the young girls at auction and use them for their own purposes as well as to cook and clean. I thank God this will not happen to me. I am to leave as soon as Papa has made arrangements with one of the mills.*"

"There's a part here I can't read," I said, frowning at a place where the ink had smeared. I looked up to find Mother, P.J., and Caleb all watching me.

"Something . . . something," I muttered as my eye skimmed down the page to a place where I could again make out the faded script. "Something . . . *was cold and I was sick,*" I continued. "*I was able to bring only the few clothes I own, my Bible, this book and the doll Mother gave me the day I left. I would not say this aloud, but truly right now I take more comfort from the little cloth doll than my Bible. I held it close to me all the way from New Dover to Lowell. I couldn't keep from crying much of the journey, but a woman took pity on me. When we arrived at Lowell, she helped me find the house where I am now staying.*

"*The people I live with are Calvin and Minna Raintree. Mr. Raintree is a manager at the mill and works in a big*" *office where we girls are not allowed to go. The Raintrees are nice to me, but I see them only after work or on Sunday when we go to church together. That is the day we do not have to work at the mill. Sometimes I see Mrs. Raintree watching me, and once she stroked my hair and told me it was a shame such a pretty girl had to leave home so young. But that made me cry because it is what my mother said the day I left.*

"The Raintrees have two children, Clara who is nine and Thomas who is only four. Clara reminds me of my sister Caroline and makes me long for home. But she is friendly and sometimes comes to the attic to talk with me."

I turned the page and looked up briefly, but no one spoke so I continued without a pause.

"December 16th. I have been in Lowell now six weeks. The work at the mill is no harder than the work at home, and the hours are no longer. We work from seven in the morning to seven at night. Most nights we must go straight from work to where we are living. They are very strict about us and make sure we do not get into trouble. They know girls so young would not be allowed to come here to work in the mills if a close eye were not kept.

"Once a week after work we have a special program we must attend, such as a preacher, an author or a politician who comes to lecture to us on 'up-lifting topics.' Usually I do not find them very interesting and often almost fall asleep. Mr. Dobbs, my overseer at the mill, escorts me home after the lectures. He also lives at the Raintrees' and has a room on the second floor much bigger than my attic room. On lecture nights, Mrs. Raintree has supper for us keeping warm on the hearth. Mr. Dobbs is not as old as Papa and has no

gray in his hair, but he is much older than I and makes me feel timid when he talks to me.

"Because I am the only mill girl staying at the Raintrees', I have a room of my own in the attic. Most of the other girls live together in what is called a dormitory *near the mill. I am lucky to have a room of my own but not so lucky to live by myself. It is easier for the girls in the dormitory to make friends. So far I have none."*

"Poor thing," Mother murmured, but by now I was so caught up in Evaline's story I barely heard her. It was as if Evaline was in the room with us and my voice was her voice.

I turned the page and stopped in dismay, then flipped through the last few pages. None of it was decipherable. All of it was a blur of washed-out blue.

CHAPTER 6 ∽

I HELD UP the book for the others to see. Little washed-out rivers of dried ink ran down the wrinkled paper. "Look," I groaned.

"Now we'll never know what happened to her!" P.J. wailed, sounding close to tears. I couldn't blame him. I felt cheated, too, as though somehow Evaline Bloodsworth's misfortune had become mine.

"How many more pages were there?" Caleb asked.

"Three," I said, "but the paper was thin so she only wrote on one side."

"Then there couldn't have been too much more."

"No, but it's still disappointing." I would have felt cheated if it had been only one page.

"Poor Evaline," Mother said softly, shaking her head. "And only twelve. What a heart-wrenching experience for one so young." She turned to me. "I wonder if she started a new book when she finished this one?"

"Well, if she did, we didn't find it. All of this stuff was together," I said, indicating the little doll, the comb, and the flint. "Nothing else was in there."

"It'd be interesting to know how the book got all the way from Lowell to Plum Cove Island," Caleb said. He picked up the flint and rubbed it between his hands as though warming it.

"I wonder if Evaline brought it here herself?" I asked, trying to sort out the possibilities. "Maybe she came back home and her family moved from the coast to the island. Maybe her father decided to try fishing when the farming got so bad."

"Maybe," Mother agreed. "But they certainly couldn't all have lived in that tiny shack. That place is barely big enough for one. Two, at the most, if they didn't mind cramped quarters."

Trust Mother to consider the logic of the situation. My imagination had expanded the shack to hold a family of six or seven. But of course Mother was right.

"Which brings us right back to where we started," I said. "What happened to Evaline, and how did her diary end up in that cabin?"

P.J. picked up the little doll from the table. "Maybe this was the doll she took with her to Lowell." His glasses had slipped again, but he didn't seem to notice.

"Could be," Caleb said, "which means Evaline might have lived in that cabin. But someone's cleared everything out of there except what fell off those shelves and was hidden." He spoke as if he, too, were sifting through evidence, searching for logical conclusions.

"Well, there's no way we can find out any more tonight," Mother said. "And I'll leave it to you to solve the mystery. I'm going to bed. Good night, everyone." With a wave of her hand, she started down the hall.

Caleb stood up, stretching.

"How about a guitar lesson, Caleb?" P.J. asked, struggling to stifle a yawn.

"Tomorrow night," Caleb said, ruffling P.J.'s hair. "My brain's too numb to make my fingers move. And I bet yours is, too."

P.J. smiled up at him. "Yeah, maybe so. I guess I'll go to bed, too. G'night." He straggled down the hallway.

At the door, Caleb turned back to me. "Do you want me to get the lights?" He looked tired, and little creases furrowed his forehead.

"That's okay," I said, shaking my head. "I'll get them. I think I'll stay up a little longer."

"Well, good night then, Molly. Sleep tight."

I watched him head toward the stairs, and then drew a deep breath and closed my eyes, wondering what it was I was feeling. Since our return from the cabin, every time Caleb looked at me or spoke my name something had stirred in the pit of my stomach, a constriction of the muscles that quickened my breath. I wasn't sure if it was because of the secret we shared or because, instead of being apprehensive of his dark, hidden side as I had been the day before, I was feeling a growing attraction to it. I wanted to lay bare whatever it was that brought that haunted look to his face, just as I wanted to discover the fate of Evaline Bloodsworth.

I thought of the boys I had casually dated in New York. Even without Caleb as a comparison, they had seemed young and very predictable, with no hidden surprises to intrigue me as Caleb did. As I watched him limp slowly up the stairs now, I savored those feelings inside me but knew I would keep them hidden from Mother, like one of the secret sins Caleb had mentioned to P.J.

I waited, listening, until I heard the door to the attic close.

Alone in the kitchen I looked down at the faded and worn cloth book. I opened it and read it through again, reading each page slowly until I came to those last blurred, unreadable pages. I closed my eyes, letting thoughts drift. The image of a young girl came to mind, a girl standing barefoot on the rocks, long skirt blowing around her legs. A girl of perhaps twelve who looked as if she could have stepped out of the last century. In my mind I saw the open door of the cabin and the little chair rocking back and forth. The images came together with a name. Evaline. I tried to push away the thought that clung, but it wouldn't let me go.

No, I told myself. It isn't possible. But the thought persisted, nagging me until I acknowledged it. If the girl on the rocks was Evaline, then since she couldn't be alive, it could only be her ghost we had seen there and later felt in the cabin. I shook my head in disbelief. Ghosts don't really exist. That's only in books or movies.

In my mind I could convince myself of the truth of that conclusion. But in some place deeper than the mind that I can only call the heart, I felt sure Caleb and I had encountered the presence of Evaline Bloodsworth in the cabin. We had seen her on the rocks in the fog. We had seen her as she must have looked as a young girl before she left New Dover to make the long, lonely journey to Lowell. But what had happened to her there? What had brought her back to New Dover and from there to Plum Cove Island?

Slowly I unloaded the dishwasher and looked at my watch. It was only ten o'clock, but I felt tired. One by one I turned out the lights and went up to bed, leaving the upstairs hall light burning in case Caleb decided to take another midnight walk.

As soon as my head touched the pillow, I fell into a deep sleep, interrupted by a series of strange dream images, brief flickers like a sputtering candle flame. I half awoke and the images faded. Then I drifted back to sleep and deeper into dream. This time it was vivid and whole.

In my dream I enter a strange hospital in some unfamiliar town. I've come to the hospital to give birth to a baby, but first I have to find the right delivery room. I must get there on time or the baby that's born won't be mine. The hospital seems deserted. No one's there for me to ask the way. I start down the empty corridor, a long, white hallway with swinging doors at either end. When I get to the end, I push through the doors only to find myself in another empty corridor. But I know I must keep searching, and quickly, or I'll lose my baby.

In the distance, I hear faint voices. I start running, desperate to arrive on time. I begin to sob, frantically following the sound of the voices around a corner and down another hallway. The voices grow stronger, and I know if I can just find the room where they are, I'll be all right. At last I reach a doorway. Throwing it open, I stumble breathless into a brightly lit delivery room. In the center of the room, under a light that dangles overhead, stands an operating table surrounded by doctors and nurses. With a sudden rush of relief, I know I've reached the right room.

But as I approach, I see a woman stretched out on the table. A doctor stands at the foot. He turns toward me, and I see he is holding a newborn baby upside down by its feet. The baby cries, and in that instant I know I've arrived too late. My baby has been born to someone else, and I've lost it forever. I burst into tears.

Within the dream I fought to come to consciousness. I

awoke slowly, filled with an overwhelming sense of loss. I was lying on my stomach, face down on my pillow. It was wet, but whether from sweat or tears, I couldn't tell. My eyes were closed, the dream still vivid in my memory, and I felt as though my heart had been ripped out of me, leaving a terrible emptiness inside.

I lay there motionless a long time, afraid of drifting back to sleep while the dream was still so vivid. Gradually it began to fade. Still tense, I let my eyes fall closed but didn't fall back into sleep. Lying awake in the darkness, I heard my door creak. Slowly I opened my eyes again. A shaft of light from the hallway cut a path across the rug.

A figure stood in the doorway, bathed in shadow with the light behind it. The figure was slight, like a child, and at first I thought it was P.J. I started to ask what he wanted, but then I realized it wasn't a boy but a young girl. She was dressed in a long, gray skirt. A white cap was tied beneath her chin. She was filmy, not quite solid, like something translucent with the light filtering through it. She started to move toward me, not walking but gliding smoothly, her bare feet not quite touching the floor.

I lay there, unable to move or utter a sound, watching as she slowly crossed the room to my bed. I was still on my stomach, my arms and hands pinned under my own weight, and I couldn't move to free them. I tried to call out but no sound came. It was like one of those dreams where you're pursued by something unseen and your legs won't move but seem to melt beneath you like butter. Only this time I was awake.

As she stood over the bed, the back of my neck prickled. Goosebumps crawled up my arms, but still I couldn't move or cry out. I tried to see her face, but with the light behind her, it was in darkness, without features. All I could see was the white cap framing the face and a fall of pale hair curling across her shoulders. My heart was pounding so hard I could feel the arm beneath my stomach jump with each beat.

Without moving or turning my head I stared up at her out of the corner of my eye. Gradually my eyes adjusted to the dark, but with the light shining from behind, she remained lost in the shadows. Only her eyes glowed large and dark against a pale face.

The figure moved slightly, and across my back I felt the same displacement of air I had felt in the cabin that afternoon, like a breeze moving against the skin.

I took a long breath and forced my lips to form words. "Are you Evaline?" I tried to ask, but the words came out only a faint whisper, and she didn't answer.

"What do you want?" I whispered again, but again there was silence.

Gradually the movement stilled. With a sound like a sigh, she turned from the bed and crossed the room to the door. She disappeared behind it, and a second later the door swung shut.

I lay awake for what seemed like a long time, but whether it was minutes or hours I couldn't be sure. I thought about getting up, but each time I started to move, a strange inertia washed over me and I stayed where I was, moving only enough to free my arms.

Outside, the sound of the ocean seemed distant. The wind sighed through the two pine trees that stood guard at either end of the front veranda. Not daring to close my eyes, I lay listening to the night sounds until at last I fell into a deep, dreamless sleep. This time I didn't awaken until light struck my eyes and I opened them to discover it was morning.

CHAPTER 7 ∾

I LAY WITHOUT MOVING, staring up at the ceiling. Memories of the night before sifted slowly through my brain like grains of sand, until each one fell into place, separate and distinct, in the order they had occurred. Remembering the dream called up again the aching sense of loss I had felt when I awakened in the middle of the night.

Then, like a slow-motion movie, I replayed in my memory the strange scene that had taken place after my dream — the girl appearing in my doorway and coming to stand over me. In the bright light of morning, I wondered if that too might not have been a dream. But it had been more real than any dream, although it was hard to explain the difference even to myself.

But why had the girl come to my room? What was it she had wanted? The questions left me with a heavy anxiety.

I blinked my eyes against the sudden shaft of sunlight that sliced across the room through the half-opened slats of the blinds. Turning my head to escape the light, I glanced at the clock beside my bed. Six-forty-five. Still early. Too early for the others to be up, I thought. But then I heard faint movements above me and the sound of a drawer closing. Caleb was up.

I dove out of bed and into the shower in the bathroom connecting my room and P.J.'s. By the time I had towel-dried my hair, thrown on some clothes, and hurried out of my room, there was no sign of Caleb. The door to the attic stood open. I ran downstairs in time to see Caleb through the front window, limping down the drive with his cane. This time I followed him, trotting down the grassless stretch of dirt in quick pursuit. He heard me behind him and turned to wait at the end of the drive.

"Do you mind some company?" I asked, breathless more from nervousness than from the run down the drive.

"Depends on the company." He looked at me with a half smile that wasn't clearly either an acceptance or a refusal, and for an instant I hesitated. "Come on along," he said and took my elbow to reinforce the invitation. As he turned left out of the driveway in the direction of Windhover, I fell into step beside him.

"Where are you going?" I asked.

"Nowhere in particular. I'm supposed to walk as much as possible and I haven't done a whole lot of it in the past few days. So I thought maybe I'd try to walk down to town." He glanced at me sideways, and I was suddenly aware of my still-damp hair hanging limply down my back. "I'll tell you what. . . . " he said.

"What?" I asked and looked down at my big toe poking through a rip in my canvas sneaker.

"If I make it all the way to town, I'll buy you a cup of coffee."

"Deal," I said with a laugh. "But going down is the easy part. It's the coming back up that might be a problem."

I was dying to tell him right away about Evaline coming to my room — for by now I was certain the girl had been Evaline — but even with all the other things that had happened I was afraid the story would sound too fantastic to be anything but a dream. I couldn't bear the thought of Caleb not believing it had really happened, maybe even joking about it.

"Did you discover any more clues about Evaline in her book?" he asked suddenly.

Startled, I wondered if he had somehow read my mind.

"No," I answered slowly, concentrating on kicking a stone along the road in front of me. "No clues. But something strange happened last night. I mean really weird."

"Oh? What was that?"

"Well, first I had this really strange dream," I said and told the dream exactly as I remembered it.

When I had finished, he gave a low whistle.

"But that's not all," I said. "That was only the beginning." Deciding to risk telling him the rest of the story, I took a deep breath and began to relate the whole strange episode. How I had heard my door open and seen a figure in the lighted doorway. How at first I had thought it was P.J. but then recognized the girl on the rocks dressed in her long skirt and white cap.

Caleb stopped walking and stared at me. "Hey," he said, "let's sit down a minute."

We sat together on a boulder at the top of the rocky rise that ran down to the water's edge. Although the sun was shining, the waves broke high on the rocks, restless and whitecapped, a reminder of the stormy sea of two days ago.

"Now tell me the rest," he said when we were seated.

I began again at the point where the girl crossed the room

toward me, gliding, not walking, in the path the light cast across the floor. I didn't call her Evaline to Caleb although that's how I thought of her. I told him how the room was light enough to see everything clearly except for her face, which had remained in shadow.

I hesitated again, afraid he might laugh when I told him how she moved to my bed and stood over me.

But he didn't laugh, not even when I told him I hadn't seen her face clearly but could tell she was young, no more than twelve or thirteen. I told him about my feeling of panic and the sense of feeling wind on my back as I had that afternoon. And finally I told him how she had disappeared again into the hallway, letting the door swing closed behind her.

I waited for his response, for the look of disbelief that would tell me he thought it all was just part of my dream. But for a long time he sat silent, staring at the ocean. When he finally spoke, he said exactly what I had been so sure of all along.

"She must be Evaline, and for some reason she wants us to know she's here."

"Then you don't think I'm crazy — or that I was just dreaming?"

"No, I don't." He picked up a piece of driftwood and hurled it down the rise, making me flinch as it bounced from rock to rock and came to rest at the water's edge.

"I've never told anyone this, Molly," he continued, "but one night right after my father died I woke up and saw him sitting in the corner of my room. He was just sitting there the way I remembered him, his pipe in his mouth, his chin resting in his hand."

I looked at Caleb in silence. The sunburn had faded to a

light shade of tan, and a sprinkle of freckles had sprung to life across the bridge of his nose. He looked healthier than the day he arrived — was it only two days ago? — but in the bright morning light, dark smudges still marked the hollows beneath his eyes.

"Dad spoke to me," he continued. "He said, 'I want you to know it's all right, Caleb. It's all right.' That's all. Then he disappeared. I was only fourteen and I never told anyone — not even Mother — because I was sure she'd say I'd been dreaming. After a while, I began to think maybe he had been a dream. But then I saw him again . . . eight months ago, when I got shot up."

Caleb took a deep breath. "I was lying on the ground waiting for a medic. I knew I was in pretty bad shape, but I was still conscious. This time he appeared and sat on the ground beside me. He said, 'It's not time yet, Caleb.' And I knew I was going to live and that I'd make it home."

Caleb gave a sharp laugh. "Of course, I still didn't know whether or not I'd be coming home with legs or with two stumps, so right then I wasn't sure his message was one I wanted to hear. But I guess there are worse things in life than losing your legs." He looked down at me. "So here I am. Legs and all."

He pushed his legs straight ahead of him and we both stared at the faded blue of his jeans. His eyes glinted in the sunlight. I wanted to touch him, to reassure him somehow, but I didn't dare.

"So," he said at last, getting up stiffly from the rock. "Your story sounds very believable to me. But I doubt if too many other people would believe us."

He held out his hand to pull me up and I took it. His fingers were cool and gripped my hand firmly.

63

"Are you sure you want to go all the way to town?" I asked.

"You owe me a cup of coffee."

"I thought it was the other way around," I said with a smile.

"You can't blame a guy for trying," he said, letting go of my hand but returning the smile. It was the first time he had smiled directly at me since his arrival, and I felt its warmth all the way down to my toes.

As we headed down the hill into town, the houses became more numerous, the lots smaller, until finally at the bottom of the hill the road leveled out and the houses gave way to shops. Caleb walked slowly, pausing to peer in windows and up narrow alleys that wound off the main street to the left. To the right lay the harbor with its fishing docks.

Except for a few dories, the docks were empty. The fishing boats would have chugged out long before sunrise and in another few hours would be rounding the end of the cove out of deep water, heading for home. Beyond the docks and the public beach, the rocks began again, a jagged procession running up the opposite curve of the cove. It was a scene I never tired of drawing, each time discovering something I hadn't noticed before.

Near the docks the pungent smell of seaweed, salt, fish, and diesel fuel filled the air. I inhaled deeply.

"Eau de old fish," Caleb joked, but he, too, took a deep breath. "If someone could bottle that smell and sell it to the tourists, he'd make a fortune."

"How does Windhover look to you?" I asked. "I don't remember it all that well. Has it changed much?"

"No, not much. Some new buildings, like you said, but basically it's the same. Except it all looks more prosperous.

Like everything's been spruced up, gotten a new coat of paint. Times must be better here. Ten years ago things were pretty rough. I imagine more than a few businesses changed hands."

We passed the True Value hardware and Ralph's Full Service, the only gas station in town. It was deserted except for a single attendant changing the price on the gas pumps. Caleb paused to watch him.

"That hasn't changed," he said with a short laugh. "The age-old ritual of raising gas prices for the summer tourists. Now I know I'm back."

He stood there for a moment, staring into the distance, seemingly lost in thought. Finally he turned to me. "You know," he said slowly, "as long as we're in town, there's somebody we should look up."

"Who's that?"

"Do you remember Dwayne and Joel Bockman?"

"Sure," I said. I remembered them well. They had always been with Caleb. I'd had a crush on Dwayne, who had stuck up for me when Joel and Caleb chased me with jellyfish.

"We should see if their grandfather's still around. He's lived here all his life, and if Evaline Bloodsworth ever lived here, he might know something about her."

"Is he still alive?" I asked with growing excitement at the thought we might learn more than what Evaline had revealed in her diary.

Caleb walked over to the gas station attendant, a boy of about my age with a cowlick and almost no chin. "Do you know if Harry Bockman is still on the island?" Caleb asked him.

"As of about an hour ago he was," the attendant replied without looking around.

"Where was that?"

"In front of the ship's chandlery. That's where he is this time every morning." The boy gave Caleb a perfunctory glance and turned back to the pump.

"Thanks," Caleb called over his shoulder as we started down the street.

We rounded the corner and walked the block leading to the waterfront. In front of the chandlery, an elderly man I wouldn't have recognized was sitting on a barrel mending a lobster trap. Other traps were piled helter-skelter at his feet. His hands were so gnarled, his knuckles so knobby, it was hard to believe he could mend anything. But his fingers wove the heavy twine into the netting at the end of the trap as deftly as Caleb played his guitar.

Caleb stopped in front of him. "Mr. Bockman," he said softly.

The man looked up from under the brim of his cap, squinting against the sun, his eyes heavy with creases that ran in ridges across his lids and down his sunburned cheeks.

"Ayuh," he acknowledged. He peered at Caleb, nodding and pointing as recognition dawned. "You're the McLaughlin boy."

"Yes, sir. Caleb McLaughlin."

"I'll be damned. For a minute there I thought I was looking at your pa, you're so like him. Are you living here now?"

"No, just here for a visit. We've been living in New Hampshire ever since Mother remarried."

"Is that so? We was all mighty sorry to hear the news about your dad. A fine gentleman. Quiet in his way, but always with a word for everyone. It was a real shock to hear. . . . " He shook his head. "Your dad never should've left the island."

66

"You're right," Caleb agreed quietly.

"It was hard here on the island then, but we all woulda helped as best we could."

"I appreciate that, Mr. Bockman. And Dad would've too. But he couldn't have asked for that."

"No, I suppose none of us could. It's good to have you back, son. There's not a time I go past your house but that I don't think of you — and your dad." He frowned. "It's hard to see someone else in the old place. Nothin' but summer folk living there since your family sold it. And none of them have kept it more'n a few years. It's standing empty again now."

"That's what I heard," Caleb said, his mouth tightening.

"Seems a shame. But you be sure and come by the house now you're here. Mildred will be tickled to see you."

"And your grandsons?" Caleb asked. "Are they still here?"

"Dwayne moved off-island to Gloucester some years ago. His wife being from Boston, she wanted to be closer to home. But Joel's still here." He threw back his head and gave a whooping laugh from deep in his barrel chest. "I remember you two giving your mas fits with all the scrapes you got into together. Joel will be glad to know you're back."

"What's he doing these days?"

"Fishing with his father. They take the boat out together."

"Joel and I kept in touch for a while," Caleb said, "but neither of us was too good about writing letters. Is he married?"

"Not so's I noticed," Mr. Bockman said with a chuckle. "But that might change if the right girl was to come along." He shifted his eyes in my direction, shading them with his hand and squinting up at me. "So who's this pretty little thing you got with you? Or are you keeping her all to yourself?"

I took a step forward and held out my hand. "I'm Molly Todd, Mr. Bockman. Caleb's cousin." His hand swallowed mine, the calluses scraping against my palm. "You wouldn't remember me, but I remember you from when I was little — and your grandsons, too. I had a crush on Dwayne back then."

"Molly Todd, huh?" he said, still peering at me from under the hood of his fingers.

"I guess Dwayne didn't wait for me to grow up," I added, laughing. "It's my loss."

"I think he might be right sorry, too. Where're you staying, Molly?"

"Mother bought that new house on Cliff Road, about halfway between town and High Point."

"Ayuh, I know the place. I heard it had sold."

"We wanted to ask you something about it," Caleb said.

"What's that?" Mr. Bockman spit into his hands and rolled a piece of the twine between his palms.

"Were you aware there was an old log cabin out in the woods at the back of the property?" Caleb asked. He shifted his weight to his left leg, leaning into the cane.

Mr. Bockman nodded his assent. "I guess I knew it once, but I'd kinda forgotten about it. Why?" He looked up at us with narrowed eyes, squinting into the sun.

"We thought you might know something about a girl — or woman — who might have lived there at one time. Her name was Evaline Bloodsworth."

Mr. Bockman stared up at us and then bent over his strand of rope. "I know something of her," he said slowly. "But mostly all I know is what I heard my grandma tell when I was little and the grown-ups warned us not to go there. I think they was mostly trying to scare us so we wouldn't use the place for things we shouldn't be doin'."

"What was it they warned you about, Mr. Bockman?" I asked, unable to stay quiet any longer.

He looked at me a long time before answering. "Well, I don't set much store by local gossip, but since you're living on the place now, I wouldn't want to be the one to put notions into your head."

"What notions?" I persisted. "Please, Mr. Bockman, we'd really like to know."

He must have read in my face that it was important to me, because this time he gave me a direct answer.

"Word was, the place was haunted."

I stared at him. "Haunted?"

"That's what some used to say. By old Evaline Bloodsworth's ghost. But as I said, that's just a story that went around here years ago and then was pretty much forgotten. Evaline was somebody folks around here wouldn't talk about." He picked up a lobster pot and threaded one end of the twine through a hole in a wooden slat. "No, sir," he continued, "I can't say I hold much belief in such things. And if you want to rest easy, you won't either."

"I never heard that story, Mr. Bockman," Caleb said with a puzzled look. "The whole time I lived here, I never heard that."

"I guess by the time you kids come along the notion had pretty much died down. And the ones still here who might have known about it got kind of tight-mouthed, especially the chamber of commerce and the realtors. They had big ideas about making Windhover into another Bar Harbor, and word of a ghost wouldn't have helped their plans any."

"Did Evaline Bloodsworth live there alone?" Caleb asked.

"Far as I know she did. From what my ma used to say, no one much would go near the place."

"Why?" I asked.

"I can't tell you, Miss Molly. I suppose my grandmother might have known, but she always said it was a story best allowed to die a natural death. Just like Evaline herself."

"Then she wasn't murdered or anything?" I said.

"No, nothin' like that. Far as I know, she died of natural causes. But I can't tell you more'n that. Except after she died word went around her ghost come back to haunt the place."

"Did anyone see her?"

"One or two claimed they did. But mostly people said they heard her crying. A terrible sound. Sad enough to break your heart."

I held my breath, knowing Caleb would ask the question.

"Those who said they saw her — what did they say she looked like? Was she a young girl with light hair wearing a white cap?"

"A young girl?" Mr. Bockman looked at us in surprise. "No, sir, she weren't a young girl. The way I heard it, those who thought they saw Evaline walking say she looked just like she must have looked at the time she died. Not a young girl at all. An old lady. All bent over, they said, with long, white hair blowing in the wind."

CHAPTER 8 ∾

W E WALKED THE half block to the Koffee Kup and sat at a table for two by the window overlooking the harbor. Caleb faced the northern curve of the cove where he had once lived. Out of the bright sunlight he looked less worn, but I had misgivings about the walk back up the hill.

I waited for him to mention the old woman, but it was clear his attention was elsewhere. His eyes were fixed on a spot halfway up the hill that could only be his old house.

"When you told me about seeing an old woman on the rocks," I said, broaching the subject myself, "I thought it must have been the fog. I should have known you were right. What Mr. Bockman said pretty much proves it was an old woman you saw."

Caleb's eyes stayed fixed on the spot on the hill.

"So the old woman and the young girl must both be Evaline Bloodsworth," I continued. "The young girl must be Evaline before she went to Lowell, and the old woman must be Evaline right before she died. But we still don't know what happened to her in between."

I paused, but getting no response, I hurried on. "I just wish we could find out how long she stayed in Lowell and if she came back to New Dover. And if she did go home to New Dover, why do you suppose she came here to Plum Cove Island? Especially considering the fact that people around here didn't seem to want anything to do with her. I mean, Mr. Bockman said they wouldn't even talk about her."

I stopped abruptly. Blabby again. The thought of my father's nickname for me made me suddenly miss him. After the divorce, he had moved to Chicago, and P.J. and I only got to see him twice a year — a week at Christmas and a week at the end of the summer before school started. We talked to him every week on the phone, but it wasn't the same. I wished he were here on the island with us, and I wished especially that he and Mother had never gotten divorced even though, by the end, they were either arguing or not speaking to one another. And whenever one of them did speak, the other automatically disagreed. Mother accused Daddy of trying to force her into a mold she didn't fit, and Daddy accused her of making her needs more important than his. I figured they were both partly right and hoped they would find a happy medium, but neither gave in. Still, I wished Daddy wasn't so far away. Sometimes it seemed like halfway around the world.

Caleb's eyes shifted from the window to something behind me, and I turned to see a waitress approaching the table with two glasses of ice water. She was a year or two older than I, attractive enough in a flashy kind of way, I had to concede. Her eyelids were heavily shadowed with mauve. Her lashes, almost as long as P.J.'s, were layered with mascara, and she had curled them. A name tag on the pocket of her blouse said her name was Peggy Ann.

After greeting us, she asked if we wanted to see menus or were we ready to order?

"Just coffee and a cinnamon roll," Caleb replied.

"And you?" she said to me without taking her eyes off Caleb. I might as well have not been there.

"The same," I said. I watched her walk away, her ample hips swinging her blue dirndl skirt. "Well," I said, "you've certainly made a conquest."

"Her? No, not my type. A bit too fleshy. And I hate white lipstick. It makes girls look like ghouls."

Before I could comment further on Peggy Ann, she reappeared with our coffee and rolls.

"Here for the summer?" she asked as she set cups and saucers and a plate with the two rolls on the table.

"More or less," I replied.

"You're earlier than most," she said to me, then turned back to Caleb. "Right now things are pretty slow."

"Do you live on the island?" Caleb asked, stirring cream and sugar into his coffee.

"Yeah, about six years now."

"Then we just missed one another," Caleb said. "I moved away nine years ago."

"Wouldn't you know. Just my luck. Can I get you anything else?"

"Just the check, I guess," Caleb said.

She laid the check beside him. "You can pay the cashier on your way out." She started away, then turned and smiled at Caleb over her shoulder. "You be sure and come again."

"Now there's an open invitation if I ever heard one," I said. "Next time you better leave me home."

"Not on your life," he said, smiling. Then after a moment

his face turned somber. "You're my protection," he said. "You help keep the demons away."

I looked up to find his green eyes watching me, dark and serious. Flustered, I bent my head and took a long sip of coffee, wondering why it was I either talked too much or couldn't think of anything at all to say.

"Do you think we'll ever find out what happened to Evaline?" I finally asked. "Talking to Mr. Bockman makes me want to know more than ever why she came here — and why she's making herself known to us now."

"I think if we learn one, we'll discover the other," Caleb said. "I mean," he went on, "if we can find out what happened after her diary ended, then we'll know why she's here now and what she wants."

We were talking about Evaline as though she were still living. In fact, she seemed almost as alive to me as if she were sitting with us at the table, drinking coffee. That idea struck me as being so close to the truth, it made me suddenly shiver.

"But if Mr. Bockman doesn't know any more about her," I said, "who around here would? He must be about as old as anybody still living on the island."

"Something will turn up sooner or later," Caleb said. "Remember, we've got the rest of the summer to find out."

Hearing him say "the rest of the summer" made me think that if Caleb prolonged his stay on the island, it would be Evaline I had to thank. The thought made her seem less ominous somehow.

We finished our coffee and rolls, and while Caleb paid the bill, I glanced at the local announcements and notices posted on the bulletin board by the door. The Koffee Kup was as good as the local paper.

"Look," I said, pointing to one of the notices as Caleb joined me. "Next Monday Bucks Harbor is having a Fourth of July celebration with fireworks and a carnival."

"P.J. will like that," Caleb said, reading over my shoulder.

"Me, too. I love carnivals and fireworks."

"Good. Then we'll all go."

"But that's not all," I said as my finger moved down the page. "On Saturday the sixteenth, there's going to be a folk festival over in New Dover, and Judy Collins is going to be there. I'd love to hear her in person." The farther I read, the better it got. "And look. Before she goes on, anyone who can play or sing is invited to perform. We could all go and you could take your guitar. P.J. would love it, and I bet even Mother would go. It'd be fun, don't you think?"

Caleb studied the brightly colored printed sheet. "Maybe so," was all he said, but I wasn't discouraged. I'd enlist P.J. to help convince him, and Mother, too, if necessary. And in the meantime, in just one more week we had the Fourth of July in Bucks Harbor to look forward to.

We started back up the hill, but before we had gone more than a quarter mile, I knew walking to town had been a mistake. Even though Caleb was using his cane for support, with each step his right leg dragged a little more.

A few hundred yards behind us, I heard a car shift gears as it started up the hill.

"Let's hitch a ride," I said quickly. Before Caleb could reply, I turned and stuck out my thumb, motioning in a direction up the hill. What I thought had been a car turned out to be a rusted-out old Chevy pickup in need of a new muffler, but to my relief it pulled over on the shoulder and stopped.

"Where you headed?" the driver asked through the rolled-down window. He was completely bald. No hair, no eye-brows, nothing. In the sunlight, the top of his head gleamed like polished pink marble.

"Halfway up the hill," I said, trying not to stare. On the seat beside him sat the biggest dog I had ever seen, a huge black Newfoundland that returned my stare with a look of complete indifference.

"Hop in the back," the man said. "Just rap on the window when we get to where you want to get out."

Caleb and I crawled into the rear, and I clambered over a pile of canvas and coils of rope to a place directly below the back window so I could signal when we got to the house.

Caleb leaned back against the side of the truck's bed and stretched out his leg. "This was a good idea, Molly," he called over the clatter of the engine. "Sure beats walking. My leg would never have made it."

I was relieved to know I hadn't offended him with my not-very-subtle maneuver.

When we neared the house, I leaned over and rapped on the window. The man pulled over, and Caleb and I scrambled down.

"Thanks a lot," we called together. The man waved, shifted into low, and rumbled on up the hill.

"Where have you two been?" Mother called from the veranda as we started up the drive. "I was beginning to get worried. Both of you gone, no note, and no way of telling when you'd left or where you'd gone."

"Sorry, Aunt Libby," Caleb said before I could answer. "It was my fault. I was going for a walk and invited Molly for a cup of coffee. We ran into Mr. Bockman in town, and I guess the time got away from us."

Mother appeared satisfied but gave me a funny look as I

went past her into the house. "And since when are you such an early riser, Molly?" she asked.

"The sun woke me," I said, telling the truth and at the same time avoiding the need to bring up the strange events of the night before.

"Well, Mrs. Pattishaw is here," Mother continued, "and I need you to collect all the dirty sheets off the beds. She's already started on the towels and she'll be ready for the sheets next."

"Okay, okay," I said, wondering why she sounded so annoyed. "I'll get them right now."

Mother had arranged with the realtor to have Mrs. Pattishaw come once a week during the summer to clean and do laundry. Her husband owned one of the fishing boats, and she cleaned houses for summer people to "set by," as she called it, for the "lean years."

Mrs. Pattishaw had been to the house the week before, and I knew she had also known Caleb when he was a young boy growing up in Windhover. I could hear her in the kitchen now, laughing and carrying on like he was her long-lost son. Before Caleb's arrival, I hadn't given any thought to the number of people in Windhover who would remember him and want to spend time with him. Now I hoped the list wouldn't grow too long. Peggy Ann had made me realize I didn't want to have to share him — not with anybody.

Upstairs, I pulled the sheets off the beds in the three second-floor bedrooms and then started up to the attic, feeling suddenly shy about invading Caleb's privacy. The attic room was spacious and airy, with dormers running along both sides. For some reason the builder had decided to decorate the room with a flowered wallpaper, and although it wasn't at all Mother's taste, she had decided to leave it and had added organdy curtains. The room was reminiscent of a little girl's room, and it was hard to imagine Caleb among all those ruffles and flowers. But there was little sign of Caleb's presence in the room, no piles of men's underwear, or shirts or jeans lying about the room. Everything had been neatly stored in the bureau or hung in the closet.

Except for Mother's desk, the only furniture in the room consisted of a wide daybed with a small table beside it, a bureau, and an easy chair covered with fabric that matched the wallpaper. On the bureau lay a comb and brush, a square wooden box, and a five-by-seven photograph in a tortoiseshell frame. Even before I walked over to take a closer look, I could see it was a picture of Caleb and Uncle John taken by someone, probably Aunt Phoebe, shortly before they left the island.

Uncle John stood on the right looking exactly as I remembered him. With his dark russet hair and slender, muscular frame, he was the mirror image of Caleb as I first saw him the day he arrived. The only difference was the mustache and the pipe clenched between his teeth. Although I best remembered Uncle John smiling in his quiet way, in this photograph his eyes looked dark and troubled, much as Caleb's eyes often looked. His left arm was thrown lightly over Caleb's shoulders.

Caleb, at twelve, looked younger than I remembered him. At the time he had seemed much older. The two of them were standing on the rocks with the ocean behind them, and in the background rested "the great love of John's life," as Aunt Phoebe had often joked, his schooner, the *Innisfree*. She rode quietly at anchor in the cove, sails furled, white bow pointing toward shore as though she had come home to rest.

Even though I knew Mrs. Pattishaw would be cleaning up here later in the day, I wiped the dust from the glass with my shirtsleeve and carefully set the picture on the bureau. I looked at the wooden box — teak, I thought, or mahogany. It had been crafted with care and fitted with small brass hinges and a brass clasp, which was open. Although I knew I was snooping, I convinced myself that if the box held anything very private, Caleb surely wouldn't have left it sitting out. I reached down and slowly lifted the top.

Inside, the box was lined with soft, honey-colored leather. On top lay a pack of cigarettes, which surprised me because I had never seen Caleb smoke, and it seemed like a strange place to keep cigarettes.

I started to move the pack aside but hesitated as first unease and then guilt crept over me. Snooping was something I had never done before, but the box belonged to Caleb, and the fact that I suddenly yearned to touch what was his allowed me to push the guilt away.

I lifted out the cigarettes. Underneath lay the patches and ribbons he had cut off his fatigue jacket. Beside them lay the medal for his Purple Heart and the Silver Star. I picked them up, weighing them in my palm as though that could somehow give me a glimpse of what it had been like to fight over there and almost die. But the medals, silent and impersonal, held their secrets.

I was about to replace them when I glimpsed an envelope under the ribbons. Lifting it out, I saw it was a letter postmarked Montpelier, Ohio. The return address in the upper corner gave the name Jeanne Englehart and a post office box number. My thoughts jumped to the conclusion that Jeanne was some girl he had known before the war, perhaps an old girlfriend, maybe even a girl he was still in love with. A quick stab of jealousy made me reach out my hand.

Not hesitating long enough to reconsider, I slipped the letter out of the envelope and began to read:

> My Dear Caleb,
>
> I want you to know how grateful I am to you for your most thoughtful and comforting letter. When I first got word that Robert had been killed in action, I thought my heart would break. The loss of my only son coming so soon after the death of his father was more grief than I thought I could bear. Then I received your letter and it was truly a gift of grace.
>
> I can't tell you how much it has helped to hear how courageously he died. To know that he died with you beside him, calmly and with no suffering, eases both my mind and my heart more than I can ever say.
>
> Even though we've never met, Robert wrote of you so often I feel very close to you. I only pray that your own wounds heal quickly and that you will be home soon. If you ever travel west, please know that my home will always be open to you.
>
> With loving fondness,
> *Jeanne Englehart*

We had never been told the exact circumstances of Caleb's being awarded the Silver Star. Heroism on the field of battle, that was all we knew. But now I was sure it must have had something to do with him risking his own life in an attempt to save his friend Robert. No wonder Mrs. Englehart was so grateful.

As I looked down at the box, I realized I had been wrong. It did indeed hold Caleb's most private possessions. He had left it out in plain sight on his bureau because of course it never occurred to him that any of us would ever meddle in his personal belongings. And now, all because I was jealous of some unknown girlfriend, I had done the unforgivable. I had not only snooped through his things but also violated the privacy of his mail. It would have served me right if I had discovered he was madly in love with some other girl. And what bothered me most was knowing I would have hated this girl sight unseen.

As much as I wanted to push away what I was feeling, my guilt made me meet it head-on. My feelings for Caleb were growing far from cousinly. I had had plenty of crushes on boys over the years, from Dwayne Bockman when I was eight to various boys I had known in New York, but I knew what I was feeling now was different. Never before had I encountered such a desire to touch and explore what was his. And not just his belongings, I had to admit, but Caleb as well. I wasn't sure where these feelings had sprung from, but as much as they scared me, I knew I'd been waiting for them a long time.

Slowly I refolded the letter and returned it to its envelope. I slipped it back under the ribbons and medals and closed the lid of the box, remembering not to latch it.

I went over to the daybed and pulled off the spread. The bedside table was empty except for a neatly stacked pile of books. The book on top was *The Complete Poems of W. B. Yeats*. A piece of music composition paper marked a place in the book. I started to open it at that spot, then drew back my hand. I had violated Caleb's privacy enough for one day.

Turning to the bed, I picked up his pillow and lifted it to my face, burying my nose in the softness of the down filling that held the faint aroma of lemon soap. I wrapped my arms around it, pressing it to my chest as though it were his body I held tight in my arms.

It wasn't until I heard Mother impatiently call from below that I stirred from my place by the bed. I pulled back the sheet and blanket, stripping first the top sheet and then the bottom and finally the pillowcase. Gathering the bed linen in a bundle, I carried it out of the room and softly closed the door behind me.

CHAPTER 9 ∾

A S PENANCE, I stayed away from Caleb for the rest of the day. After lunch he went out on the veranda with a pile of books and stretched out on the wicker chaise. P.J. disappeared with a boy named Roger, a new friend he had discovered that morning on the rocks.

Mother left to do some shopping in Bucks Harbor, and I changed into my bathing suit and headed for our beach with my sketchbook and a towel. I tried going in the ocean, but the water was still so cold it curled my toes and numbed my ankles, so I sat on a rock to sketch, concentrating on small images — barnacles on the rocks, a broken crab shell, a strand of seaweed.

I made myself stay for an hour, then gave it up and headed back to the house. Caleb was still stretched out on the veranda, his head resting against the back of the chaise. His eyes were closed, and his book lay open on his stomach. I couldn't be sure if he was asleep or just resting, and for a moment I was tempted to join him on the porch and wait for him to open his eyes. But I walked on past the veranda and in the back door.

I didn't see him until just before supper when he came out to the kitchen, where I was making a meat loaf. Only too aware of my feelings, and knowing what I had done that morning, I couldn't meet his eyes.

"You disappeared this afternoon," he said. "Did you go somewhere?"

I shook my head, my hands immersed up to my wrists in a glop of ground meat and bread crumbs, onion, egg, and milk. "I was around," I said, "but I thought you wouldn't mind some time to yourself."

He got a beer from the fridge and opened it.

"Want one?" he asked.

I pulled my gloppy hands out of the meat loaf mixture and held them up. "Maybe later," I said with a laugh, pleased he thought of me as old enough to have a beer.

He sat on the stool by the table and sipped out of the can.

"Meat loaf?" he said, nodding at the bowl.

"Yeah. Chef's special."

He watched while I scooped the mixture into a pan and shaped it into a loaf, laying strips of bacon across the top. "You look like you know what you're doing," he said.

"When Mother had to go to work full-time, I didn't have much choice. It was either learn to cook or starve."

"I was sorry to hear about the split. I always liked both your mother and father a lot. I never did hear exactly why it happened."

"Me neither," I said. "This family doesn't talk about things like that. I think there's some law of physics that describes their marriage — about how if two things meet head-on, they'll bounce away in opposite directions. Or something like that."

Caleb tried to suppress a smile. "Something like that," he agreed. He set the can of beer on the table. "You must miss your dad."

"Yes, I do," I said, trying to swallow the lump that unexpectedly rose in my throat. Out of the blue, tears started coming out of my eyes, and I didn't know why. With my hands still covered with meat loaf, I couldn't even wipe them away, and they just kept running down my face. I tried to wipe my cheek with my shirtsleeve, but the tears kept coming, and I turned and leaned against the sink, sticking out my messy hands in front of me. I couldn't believe I was crying now, in front of Caleb, but I couldn't seem to stop.

Caleb came and stood behind me. With one hand he reached around and took my chin. With the other, he took the dish towel and wiped my eyes and cheeks.

"Hey," he said softly, "I'm sorry. I didn't mean to make you cry. What a klutz."

I shook my head and took a deep, gulping breath. "No," I said, "it's not you, it's me. I'm the one that's the klutz." I attempted a shaky laugh. "I don't usually do that. My God, they've been divorced for seven years. You'd think by now I'd be able to deal with it."

"You were only ten when they split," he said, letting go of my chin. His hand came to rest lightly on my shoulder. "That's a bad age for a girl to lose her father."

I stood very still, hardly breathing, aware of the touch of his hand, afraid if I moved he might move, too. His fingers felt firm and warm through the thin cotton of my shirt.

"Feeling better now?" he asked.

I nodded, and looked up at him. His eyes held a puzzled look, almost surprise, and for a moment I thought — hoped — he might kiss me. But he took a step backward, lifted his hand from my shoulder, and turned back to the stool.

Taking a deep, quavering breath, I turned on the faucet

to rinse my hands. "Anyway," I said at last, "I guess there's no good age to lose a father. It's no worse for a girl at ten than a boy at fourteen."

I turned to face him. We had all avoided the subject of Uncle John ever since Caleb came. I knew Mother wouldn't say anything. She made a point of never talking about Uncle John. Now it seemed the least I could do was let Caleb know how sorry I was.

"I shouldn't complain," I went on, plunging ahead. "At least I've still got my father. I mean, at least he's not dead. It must have been much worse for you. I was really sorry, you know," I finished lamely.

Caleb moved the beer can in slow circles on the tabletop. "Yeah, that wasn't a good year for fathers, was it?"

"Being here on the island probably doesn't help, either," I said. "It must remind you. You know. With all the people telling you how much you look like him."

"That doesn't bother me," he said slowly, "as much as thinking about the other ways I might be like him. The genes in our family seem to run strong."

"The genes?" I repeated.

"They make us who we are in more ways than just our looks," he said. "You have the artistic gene. I have his look-alike genes. I also seem to have gotten his personality, and sometimes I think about what it would be like to get that depressed. I wonder if someday I might ever . . . you know, feel that bad."

I couldn't believe what he was hinting at. I stared at him in growing horror. This was far more than I had bargained for. But I couldn't seem to do anything except stand there and shake my head.

"No, Caleb," I said at last, "you can't mean that. You

could never do that. That's not a gene. That's giving up hope. That's just having things get so bad you don't think they're going to get any better."

My whole body stiffened, recoiling at the idea that he had even been thinking about suicide. Nothing in this world was worth such a thought. Why had I ever mentioned fathers in the first place? I could feel my head going back and forth like a puppet out of control.

"You don't inherit that," I went on, my voice rising. "You can always make your own choice on that. And besides, knowing how you felt when your father died, how could you even think about doing that to Aunt Phoebe *again* — or to any of us?"

I looked at his face with its straight eyebrows and nose, the cheeks that sloped down to his mouth with its firm lower lip and softly curved upper lip. The thought of his face twisted in death made me feel sick.

He looked at me. "I was the one who found him, you know."

I stared back at him. At the time of Uncle John's death, I had learned that he had killed himself with carbon monoxide. But never that Caleb had been the one to find him.

"No," I whispered, "I didn't know." How could a fourteen-year-old boy deal with something like that?

Caleb looked out the window toward the woods in the back. His eyes had that distant look again, as if some movie were playing in the back of his mind.

"That day, when I came home from school, Mother was at work," he said, his voice low and husky. "I heard the car running in the garage. I went out to look — and there he was. Sitting slumped behind the wheel, his head resting on the rim. But I was too late."

I wanted to go to Caleb, put my arms around him, and try to wipe away the memory, but I was afraid to move, afraid to show him how much I cared. So I just stood there with my arms dangling at my sides, two useless appendages.

After a moment he continued, but I could see in his eyes that he was back in his garage at that moment of discovery. "The worst of it is," he said, "that I'll never know whether he really meant to kill himself or if that was the only way he knew to ask for help."

"What do you mean?" I asked, my voice barely audible. "How could he have not meant to do it?"

"I've never said this to anyone, Molly, certainly not to Mother, but ever since he first appeared to me after he . . . after he died . . . I've wondered if he was counting on me to be there in time to save him."

"But how could that be, Caleb?"

"Because usually I took the bus to and from school every day, and it always got to our corner by three-thirty. Mother was working and didn't get home until six, but I was always home before four." He took a long swallow of beer and set the can carefully back down on the same ring of moisture. "Only that day I stayed after school to shoot baskets with a couple of friends. Dad had stayed home from work complaining of a sore throat, but I didn't call him to let him know I'd be late. By the time I'd walked home, it was almost five."

He moved the can around and around in the same wet circle. "If I'd taken the bus, I might have gotten home in time. He might have been counting on that. . . ." His voice trailed off.

I saw the anguish in his face, and I began to fathom why he seemed to shut everything out whenever his old house was mentioned, the house where he had been happy for so many years.

"But you know something, Molly?" His eyes turned from the window to look at me. "You're right about one thing. Knowing what the carbon monoxide did to him, how it made him look, I couldn't do that to anyone. Not that way."

"Not *any* way, Caleb! Not ever!"

The fierceness in my voice took Caleb by surprise, I guess, because he suddenly smiled. Nothing like a grin, but enough of a smile to erase the shadows that clouded his eyes.

"You're not a bad person to have around, Molly Todd," he said softly, and the look of surprise reflected again in his eyes.

I might have gone to him then, put my arms around him, but that was the moment Mother walked in.

"Molly, haven't you got that meat loaf in the oven yet? At this rate, it'll be midnight before we get dinner on the table." She stopped, looking first at Caleb and then at me, and then at Caleb again. "Well, you two look serious. Been solving the world's problems?"

I could tell she was trying to sound jocular, but as she passed me to turn on the oven, she gave me the same funny look she had given me that morning when Caleb and I got back from town.

"Not quite all the world's problems, Aunt Libby," Caleb said, "but give us time."

"Hmmmm," was all Mother said, but she looked at both of us again with a quizzical lift of her eyebrows. "Mashed potatoes, Molly?" she said at last. "I'll fix a salad."

"Put me to work, too," Caleb said.

"The first thing you can do is pour me a beer. Then if you want a job, you can set the table."

89

Caleb got a can of beer and a glass, poured it half full, and set it beside her. As he began collecting mats and silverware for the table, P.J. clattered up the back steps and into the kitchen. His face was smiling and rosy, and even his glasses were on the bridge of his nose where they were supposed to be.

"What's for supper?" P.J. asked.

"Meat loaf," I said, "and mashed potatoes and salad. And Mrs. Pattishaw's bread pudding."

"Yuck," P.J. said, scrunching up his face.

"Hey! That's my favorite dinner you're putting down!" Caleb said.

P.J.'s face relaxed. "Well, mashed potatoes are okay. And meat loaf's not *too* gross, I guess."

"Bread pudding's my favorite," Caleb said, and I could see that P.J. was clearly torn. His face registered momentary indecision.

"No way," he said at last. "Not bread pudding."

"Go wash up," Mother said. "It'll be ready soon."

As P.J. started for the stairs, the phone in the front hall rang and he picked it up. "Todd's poultry farm, which chicken do you want?" he said airily, then called over his shoulder, "It's for you, Mom," and kept on going.

Mother went to the phone, and her voice drifted to the kitchen from the hallway. "Are you sure it's absolutely necessary? . . . Yes, I knew it was coming, but this just isn't a good time. . . . Well, if I must, I must. As long as it's only one day. . . ."

She came back into the kitchen looking annoyed and worried. "Damn! They're moving the trial up, and they're shorthanded. I have to go to New York next week to take depositions."

90

"When?" I asked, careful not to look at Caleb.

"I have to be there early on the fifth. Which means I'll have to leave here on the Fourth to fly out of Bangor."

"That's rotten, Aunt Libby," Caleb said. "You'll miss the Bucks Harbor Fourth of July celebration."

"Are they going to have fireworks?" P.J. asked, coming back into the kitchen.

"Fireworks *and* a carnival," Caleb said.

Behind his lenses, P.J.'s eyes grew round and huge. "Great! We can still go, can't we, Mom?"

"I suppose," Mother said. "As long as you all go together." She gave me a pointed look.

"Neato. Could Roger go with us?"

"Why not?" I said with a shrug. "The more, the merrier." I shot a quick glance at Mother. "I know, I know. Don't be sarcastic." Actually, I was glad to have Roger come along. He would be a distraction for P.J.

At supper Caleb told Mother and P.J. about our conversation with Mr. Bockman.

"He said Evaline Bloodsworth died of old age. But no one on the island now remembers why she came here. She was taboo, Mr. Bockman said. The people wouldn't even talk about her."

"It's hard to figure," Mother said, "how that poor child who was sent away from home to work in the mills could have turned out to be such a pariah."

"What's a pariah?" P.J. asked.

"An outcast," Mother said. "Someone shunned by society."

"Like a scapegoat?"

"Kind of," Mother agreed, "but not for quite the same reasons."

"Roger's got a cool chemistry set, and we did experiments," P.J. said, dismissing the subject of Evaline Bloodsworth. Now that he had a real friend, his interest in her had waned.

"Well, don't blow yourselves up," Mother said with a frown.

As we were finishing supper, the phone rang again, and this time it was for Caleb.

Peggy Ann, I thought with a quick stab of jealousy. Somehow she'd found out his name and where he was staying. And now she'd probably want to hang around with him the rest of the summer. By the time Caleb got to the phone, I was silently fuming.

It turned out to be Joel Bockman, inviting Caleb to go out fishing with him and his father the next day.

"Be sure and invite him over for supper," Mother said. "We'd all like to see him again. It's been a long time."

So, I thought, P.J. has made a new friend and now Caleb has found an old friend.

I poured cream on my bread pudding and watched a single raisin float to the surface as a creeping emptiness slithered across my chest and into my throat. I thought of Evaline Bloodsworth all alone in the cabin, with no one who would even talk to her. Maybe P.J.'s interest had waned, but for me she was still a real person.

I thought of the figure I had seen in my room the night before and felt sorry for her. Perhaps in the quiet of some future night she might appear again, and this time I wouldn't respond in fear.

CHAPTER 10 ∽

A FTER SUPPER, Caleb went up to the attic to get his guitar for the lesson he'd promised P.J.

As Mother was finishing a cup of Sanka, I got Evaline's diary out of the drawer where I had stored it the night before. Idly, I glanced through it again, although by now I knew the events of those few days almost by heart. I came to the page where she talked about her arrival in Lowell, and my eye fell on the name of the people she stayed with.

"That's a strange name," I commented to Mother.

"What is?"

"Raintree. Calvin and Minna Raintree. I've never come across that name before."

"It is unusual. I wonder if any are still in Lowell? Raintrees, I mean."

"Mother, you're a genius!" I shouted, throwing my arms around her and nearly lifting her out of her chair.

"Oooff," she said with a loud exhalation. "Molly, you're going to break my ribs, not to mention the cup and saucer!"

"Who's a genius?" P.J. asked, following Caleb back into the kitchen.

"Mother is," I said with growing excitement. I looked at Caleb. "The Raintrees! Why didn't we think of them? That's who might know something about Evaline. If there are any Raintrees still living in Lowell, chances are they'd be from the same family. After all, how big is Lowell, and how many Raintrees can there be?"

"Let's find out," Caleb said, heading for the phone. "Okay, Aunt Libby?"

"By all means," Mother called after him.

While I hung over his shoulder, he dialed information and asked for Lowell, Massachusetts. Then he asked for any listings under the name of Raintree. I held my breath, bracing myself for the disappointment of hearing there were no Raintrees in Lowell at all. But when he jotted a number on the notepad and wrote the name *Jerome* beside it, my heart leapt.

He hung up the phone and looked at me with a smile that lit up his face. "Here, Molly," he said, handing me the phone and the pad with the number. "There's only one, but this was your idea. You make the call."

Nervously, I dialed long distance and asked for the number. I had no idea what I was going to say.

The phone rang four times before someone answered.

"Raintree residence," a woman's voice said, and I breathed a sigh of relief.

I cleared my throat twice and began. "My name is Molly Todd, and I'm calling from Plum Cove Island, Maine. I'm trying to get in touch with any members of the Raintree family who might have had relatives living in Lowell at the beginning of the last century." I crossed my fingers. "By any chance are you related to that family?"

I listened to her answer, drawing nervous doodles on the pad until she had finished. Then I thanked her and slowly hung up. By now, both Mother and P.J. were in the hallway with Caleb and me.

They all looked at me.

"It's them!" I shouted. "The same Raintrees who lived in Lowell a hundred and fifty years ago. Except they're out of town, and we'll have to wait until next week. That was the housekeeper. She said they were visiting relatives and wouldn't be back until after the Fourth. But she said she knows the family has lived in Lowell almost two hundred years. She said the Raintrees are one of the oldest families in town." I let out a great sigh. "Now all we have to do is wait until next week."

"And hope that they know something about Evaline Bloodsworth," Mother added. "It's possible, you know, that any record of her might have been lost long ago. Or forgotten."

I refused to even think about that possibility.

That evening, we all sat around the table in the kitchen for P.J.'s guitar lesson. Even Mother stayed. She got out a sweater she had been working on for about three years and began to knit. Outside, the sun had dropped beneath the horizon. The sky gradually faded from red-orange to salmon, then lavender, and finally to deep indigo. Through the window I could see the full moon begin its slow rise, clear and bright. Tomorrow would be a good day for fishing.

"P.J.'s got talent, Aunt Libby," Caleb said at the end of the lesson. "He's got a real knack — and the ear for it, too."

Mother nodded her head. "I'm not surprised."

P.J. tried to act nonchalant but couldn't hide the pleased

look that washed over his face, making it shine almost as brightly as the moon. This had been a good day for P.J. He deserved one.

I brought up the Judy Collins concert later in July.

"The three of us have to gang up on Caleb," I said, "and make him play."

"Let me hear you, then, Caleb," Mother said with a smile. "I can't promote someone I've never heard."

Caleb lifted the guitar to his chest, plucking each string lightly to check the tuning.

" 'Sounds of Silence,' Caleb," I requested softly, and he moved easily into the opening chords. The melody, as insistent as a heartbeat, swirled through the kitchen like a warm wind.

He began the lyric, about saying hello to darkness, his old friend, and somehow, after what he had told me earlier, the words seemed very appropriate.

I looked at Mother. Her knitting lay in her lap, forgotten. She watched him, never taking her eyes from his face.

I watched him, too, knowing that what I'd felt earlier in his bedroom, and then again before supper in the kitchen, hadn't been some momentary response. As much as I didn't want to admit it, I was falling in love with my cousin. And not just any cousin, but my double first cousin in whom the blood flowed together from both sides of my family.

As Caleb came to the end, I turned my eyes to Mother again, afraid she might read on my face what I was feeling. But her eyes were still watching Caleb with an almost puzzled look.

In the silence that followed, Caleb paused, thinking, while his fingers strummed softly. Then, slowly, quietly, he began to sing "Danny Boy," a song I vaguely remembered from when I was a child and somehow connected to Uncle John. I remembered how lovely and sad it was and thought it a good choice. But before he had sung more than the opening phrases, Mother broke in.

"No, Caleb," she said, "not that one. Please. Not tonight. It's still too painful."

P.J. looked at her in surprise, but for me her response was not unexpected. Ever since Uncle John's death, Mother had avoided reminders of him. Caleb stopped singing it right away and swung into an Irish sea chantey.

At the end, Mother pushed back her chair.

"Since I can't be here for the Fourth of July," she said, "let's plan on going to the Judy Collins concert together. Right now," she went on, "we should let Caleb get to bed. If he's going fishing tomorrow, he'll have to be up by four in the morning."

In the overhead light her face looked strangely worn and tightly drawn. She turned to Caleb. "Do you need the Jeep to get to town?"

"No, thanks, Aunt Libby. Joel said he'd pick me up. I'll try not to wake everybody."

"Don't forget to invite him for supper."

That night the four of us went upstairs together. With a brief good-night Caleb continued on up to the attic. I watched him go, half wishing I could follow. But so much had happened in the past few days, everything inside of me was all twisted up in a muddle. For once I looked forward to being alone and having a chance to sort things out. I started into my room.

"Molly," Mother said, "come into my room a second, will you?"

With an uneasy feeling I followed her into her bedroom as P.J. went into his room and closed the door.

From the way she had been looking at me all evening, I could guess what was coming and I waited with a sense of dread. I was too tired for this now. But no matter what she said, I knew I couldn't let myself get upset or emotional.

She shut the door behind us. My stomach churned like it used to when I was little and felt guilty about doing something bad even when I wasn't the one who had done it.

"Molly," she began, and from the way she said my name, I knew the worst was coming. "I don't quite know how to bring this up without just coming right out and saying it. I know it's my fault, because I *asked* you to spend time with Caleb, to stay with him. But I wasn't thinking about the fact that of course he's a man now." She paused and looked at me. "And I wasn't thinking about how very attractive he might be."

I waited, watching her. Not knowing what to say myself, I decided it would be best to let her have her say.

"But now I sense things are . . . well, that things . . . feelings . . . might get out of hand. I can see it would be hard for any girl not to fall in love with him. You two are alike in so many ways. You both seem . . . attuned. And I feel responsible." She waited for me to reply, but I kept silent. "How *do* you feel about Caleb, Molly?" she asked at last when I didn't respond.

I stared at a line in the wallpaper where the pattern of flowers didn't quite line up. "I like Caleb," I said. "Of course I like him. He's my cousin and he's a very nice person."

"Yes, but he isn't just your cousin, Molly. You two are double first cousins. That makes the blood ties close. Too close."

"Too close for what?" I countered, knowing very well what she meant since I had been thinking the same thing only a short while before.

"You know very well what I mean, Molly," she said, stating my thought as though she had read my mind. "Too close for any kind of relationship. Other than a cousinly one. In terms of blood ties, Caleb is almost like your brother."

"So?" I said. "I know that." I studied the mismatched flowers intently.

"Molly, look at me." Reluctantly, I swung my eyes around to meet hers. "Things haven't always been the easiest between us," she said. "Sometimes I don't know whether we're too different or too alike. But you're my only daughter, and above all else I don't want to see you hurt. There's been enough of that in this family. I can see you care about Caleb. And he's so vulnerable right now. . . ." She let her sentence trail off.

I took a deep breath to steady my voice. "I'm not going to get hurt, Mother. And I should care about him, shouldn't I, especially after all he's been through?" I took care to look at her directly.

"Yes, of course. But you know what I mean, Molly. As long as it's not caring too much. You just mustn't get romantically attached. It would be impossible."

Her words jabbed the pit of my stomach, but I pushed them away.

"I like having Caleb here, Mother," I said. "It's nice having somebody older to do things with instead of just P.J." I tried to give a little laugh but it came out more of a gurgle. "Good Lord, Mother, I'm certainly not going to fall in love with him or anything, so you don't have to worry."

She gave me a sharp look. "Well, I don't particularly like the idea of leaving you two alone here next week."

"We won't be alone. P.J. will be here."

"That hardly counts, Molly, and you know it. Maybe I should get Mrs. Pattishaw to come and stay while I'm gone."

I could feel my resolve about staying cool begin to fade.

"Oh, Lord, Mother! You wouldn't do that," I burst out. "You couldn't. I'm not a kid, and Caleb isn't either. You said yourself, it's only for a day. You *can't* have some *baby-sitter* in to stay with us. It would be too mortifying!"

"For goodness' sakes, Molly, there's no need to get melodramatic," Mother said, holding up her hands in surrender. "All right. I won't ask Mrs. Pattishaw. But I want you think about what I've said."

"I will, Mother, I really will," I answered in my most agreeable voice and kissed her on the cheek. "But there's nothing to worry about. Really." I looked her right in the eye.

She looked at me closely, a little frown puckering her forehead. "We'll see how things go in the next few days . . ." she said, kissing me back. Before she could finish the sentence, I escaped into the hallway and the privacy of my own room.

As tired as I was, I lay awake for a long time. I had lied to Mother. Now, over the next week, I couldn't give her even the hint of a reason to change her mind — or even worse, to send Caleb home. I would have to be very careful. I would have to keep my distance from Caleb, spend less time with him. I would have to pretend I didn't care.

But knowing how I really felt, I realized how hard that was going to be. Mother's warning had come too late.

Just before sleep finally took hold of me, my thoughts

turned from Caleb to Evaline, and I wondered if she might appear again that night. As much as I dreaded the thought of her ghostly visage coming out of the dark into my room again, for some strange reason I almost hoped she would. She could be a friend. And I would welcome a friend, I thought, as I drifted toward sleep. Even a friend who was a ghost.

CHAPTER 11 ∾

AT FOUR-THIRTY I was awakened by the flash of a headlight past my window and the sound of a car turning into the drive, pulling to a stop beside the house. Joel had arrived to pick up Caleb for fishing. A door closed, and the sound of men's voices drifted up from below.

The moon had set. In the darkness I climbed out of bed and knelt at the window. The sun had not yet started to rise, but a faint tinge of rose washed the eastern sky. Caleb and Joel stood in the headlight's beam, hands clasped, talking in lowered voices. Then Joel climbed into the driver's seat as Caleb walked around to the other side. He stopped and looked up at my window, raising his hand in silent salute. I waved back.

The early morning air was damp and chilly, but I waited by the window until the car disappeared down the hill. Then I crawled back into bed and slept until awakened by P.J. singing "Feelin' Groovy" at the top of his lungs in the bathroom.

The rest of the day dragged by. By early afternoon I had

run out of things to do, so I gathered as many art supplies as I could carry and headed for the cabin.

At the clearing, I hesitated. Without Caleb, I suddenly wasn't so sure I wanted to go into the cabin. Reminding myself that Evaline Bloodsworth was a friend, I approached the cabin cautiously and pushed open the door. I looked at the rocker, but it sat motionless. Feeling no sense of a presence, I slowly entered.

The midafternoon sun breaking across the clearing and through the window reminded me of Caleb's face, half in light, half in shadow, and I decided to try and sketch it as best I could from memory. The cabin was gloomy, but I set up the easel and pad of paper close to the window and began drawing with charcoal, closing my eyes now and then to get the image of his face vivid in my mind. At first I worked easily with no trouble, but the further I progressed the harder it became. Finally I had to give the sketch up. I had already decided to make it a parting gift at the end of the summer, but to finish it I'd have to take a good black-and-white photo of Caleb. With a sigh, I started to put the charcoal away.

Then I heard it, like an answering sigh, a sound so slight it could have been the wind through the trees. In slow motion I set my case on the floor, afraid of making too loud a noise or too abrupt a movement. She was there with me. A mist, a soft flutter of wind — no more than that — but I knew it was Evaline. I felt no rush of adrenaline, no sudden fear, only a curious companionship. The sigh came again, and it was so soft, if there'd been any other sound I'd never have heard it.

I held my breath, waiting. Nothing. Then I barely whispered her name. "Evaline?"

I waited again. "If you are Evaline, why are you here?"

Still nothing except that slight movement of air. I whispered again, so softly I could barely hear myself, "Whatever it is you want, we won't forget you."

Gradually the mist disappeared, the cabin emptied. Nothing stirred. I was alone.

*

Shortly before supper, Caleb and Joel drove up the drive. I had been reading on the veranda and waited until the car came to a stop before moving to the top of the steps to greet them. Joel was just as I remembered him nine years ago. Lanky and tall, with hair the color of bleached wheat and pale gray eyes that looked as if they, too, had been bleached from too many hours in the sun. Caleb's face and arms had darkened from his day on the water, and a new layer of freckles deepened the bronze tone of his skin. The pallor he had come with to the island was gone.

Joel stood on the step below me, eyes level with mine, hands thrust deep in the pockets of his jeans.

"Hey, Molly," he said with the wide grin that I remembered only too well signaled some prank. "How're you doin'? Still hiding under Caleb's bed to spy on us?"

I started to deny it, then glanced at Caleb, who stood nonchalantly to one side. I burst out laughing. "That's not fair," I said. "Caleb coached you! Two against one. I can see things haven't changed much."

"Well," he said, giving me an appraising look, "Caleb also told me you weren't such a snub-nosed little girl anymore. I can see he's right on that score."

"I wasn't ever snub-nosed," I protested. "An obnoxious pest maybe, but not snub-nosed!"

Joel leaned forward, peering into my face, and I caught

a distinct whiff of whiskey on his breath. They must have stopped at the Salty Dog, the only bar in Windhover. Even Caleb looked more relaxed than I had seen him since his arrival.

Whether it was because Joel was there or because both men were feeling an alcoholic glow, the evening seemed somehow festive. Over supper, we did a lot of reminiscing and laughing. I tried to look at Caleb as little as possible and made a point of flirting with Joel, hoping Mother would notice.

But at the end of the evening my strategy backfired.

As he was leaving, Joel took my hand as if to shake it but held it instead. "You've grown up real good, Molly," he said with a smile. "You should've let me know you were here last summer. I know Dwayne was always your favorite, but now that he's out of the picture, maybe we could go out sometime."

We were all standing at the front door, and I could feel Mother watching me — and Caleb, too.

"Great, Joel," I said, trying to feign enthusiasm. "That would be nice . . . sometime," I ended vaguely and withdrew my hand.

"So long for now. And thanks, Mrs. Todd." With three strides of his long legs, Joel was across the porch and down the steps. He stopped and looked back at us clustered in the doorway, and this time his face was serious. "It's good to see Caleb again," he said. "It's great you got him to come back. Now all we have to do is get him to stay."

With a quick wave of his hand, he backed his car down the drive and headed toward town. The taillights disappeared over the hill, and I wondered how in the world I could avoid going out with him without Mother getting on my case.

All evening I had waited for the chance to tell Caleb about encountering Evaline again, but by the time I turned from the door, he had already started upstairs to bed. I watched him make the turn at the top of the stairs and willed my legs not to follow.

*

The next morning, for the first time, we were all together at breakfast.

"I was thinking maybe it's time I took a last look at the house," Caleb said as we were finishing, his fingers nervously turning the saltshaker. "Would anyone like to go along?"

From the grim expression on his face, it was clear he didn't want to go alone. "Sure, that's great," I agreed. "P.J., would you like to come?" I asked quickly, knowing Mother wouldn't want Caleb to go alone either, but also wouldn't want me to be alone with him. "Why don't you invite Roger, too?"

"Roger can't do anything today. His grandparents are coming," P.J. said. "But I'll go."

At midmorning the three of us headed for the Jeep. I grabbed my camera, thinking I might get a chance to take a picture of Caleb. You know, in front of your old house, I could say to him casually.

Mother handed Caleb the keys, so I climbed in the passenger's side while P.J. crawled in back. The morning was cool, and Caleb was wearing the fatigue jacket with the missing patches. The thought of them stacked neatly in the box on his bureau made me cringe.

P.J. leaned over from the backseat, peering ahead as the road wound down toward town. He rubbed his finger over the spot below Caleb's right shoulder where one of the patches had been sewn.

"What was here?" he asked.

"Just a patch showing what my combat unit was in the army."

"What were you?"

"Officially, my job was a forward observer with the field artillery. But in-country, we all did pretty much whatever needed doing."

"Where's 'in-country'?" P.J. asked.

Caleb smiled. "That's just an expression. It means in Vietnam."

P.J. was heading into that forbidden territory of the war. I tried to shoot him a warning look, but he was concentrating on Caleb's jacket. I hoped he would shut up.

"Do you have any more patches?" he asked after a moment.

"A few, and some ribbons. But they're no big deal. Everybody got them."

"But everybody didn't get a Purple Heart and a Silver Star," P.J. said with pride. I turned and glared at him, but he was looking only at Caleb.

"No, not everybody," Caleb said. "But a lot got Purple Hearts."

"Is that the one you get for being wounded?"

"That's the one."

"How did you get wounded, Caleb?"

This time I glanced at Caleb, afraid I might see his face tighten and grow dark with those shadows that seemed to come out of nowhere. But his face was relaxed, his eyes watching the road ahead. He didn't seem to mind P.J.'s questions.

"Our platoon was on night reconnaissance, and we ran smack into an ambush. We had to go across a clearing in the jungle that had been rigged with Claymore mines —"

"What's a Claymore mine?" P.J. interrupted.

"Actually they were American mines. But then the Vietcong got ahold of them and used them against us. We used to call them 'Chinese TVs' because they looked like a little TV screen on very short legs. They were several pounds of C-4 explosive that were detonated from a distance."

He had slowed the Jeep as we passed through Windhover and now accelerated again as we started up the far hill. "We didn't know the field had been rigged," he went on, "until we got halfway across. Then mines started detonating all over the clearing. We had to retreat in a hurry. Not too many made it back."

"But you got back."

"Eventually."

"P.J., why don't you shut up?" I said, thinking of that letter lying in the bottom of the box.

P.J. looked at me in hurt surprise, his eyes large behind his lenses, which made me feel mean as well as guilty. It was Caleb who came to the rescue.

"That's okay, Molly. I don't mind telling him," he said quietly. P.J. looked relieved.

"Then what happened, Caleb?" he asked. "When were you wounded?"

"The Vietcong shot off a couple of flares. The whole clearing lit up, and they started shooting. I was almost out of the clearing when I got shot in my left leg. In the calf."

"But you got hurt real bad, Caleb. Aunt Phoebe told us."

"That was a little later."

I wondered if he was going to say anything about Robert Englehart.

"What happened later?" P.J. was nothing if not persistent.

"I made it to the other side of the clearing, but a lot of wounded men were still out there. Sitting ducks. If somebody didn't go after them, they all would have been killed."

"So you did?" P.J. asked, his voice full of awe. "Jeez, Caleb, weren't you scared?"

"Sure, but you don't have time to worry much about that."

"But if you were shot in the leg, how could you get them? Didn't you have to carry them?"

Caleb shifted into second gear as we neared the steep part of the rise beyond the cove. It was clear he remembered this stretch of road well.

"Things like that are funny sometimes, P.J. It just didn't seem to matter. By that time, I hardly felt it."

"How many men did you bring back?"

"Three." Still no mention of Robert Englehart, and of course I didn't dare ask.

Caleb went on. "My last time out, though, a mine blew up close to me. That's when I was really wounded. If I hadn't been wearing a flak jacket, I guess I might have been killed."

"How did you get out?" As much as I wanted P.J.'s questions to end, I wanted to hear Caleb's story even more, and so I stayed silent.

"By that time, I guess the Vietcong had used all their flares," Caleb answered, "and luckily it was dark again. The shooting stopped and no more mines went off. Eventually a medic found me."

"Is that why they gave you the Silver Star? For getting the men?"

"That was it. But it was no big deal either, P.J."

"Yes, it was too a big deal," I said. I had been leaning against the door, watching Caleb as he told P.J. the story.

I wanted to take his hand and hold it but instead I reached out and touched him lightly on the shoulder, just for a second. He turned and smiled at me.

Just past the top of the hill, the road cut inland, leaving a broad strip of land on the ocean side wide enough for a house. As we drew near, I glanced sideways at Caleb. This time the muscles in his neck were rigid. Returning to his old house seemed to be more of an ordeal than talking about the war.

We came up over a rise in the road and saw the house ahead. It was a stately white clapboard New England colonial with dark green shutters, perched on the crest of the hill. An old sea captain, the last on the island, had built it more than a hundred years ago. Around the top of the house ran a widow's walk with a glassed-in cupola large enough to hold someone waiting and watching for a ship to sail into the sanctuary of the harbor. It was a beautiful house, built with a sense of permanence and grace.

Long ago, Mother had told me the story of how Uncle John came to own the house. The sea captain's son inherited it and lived there for many years, but his wife died young, and he never remarried or had any children. In his wanderings along the coast, he met Uncle John and gradually grew to think of him as the son he never had. When he died, he left the house to Uncle John because, as he stated in his will, he knew Uncle John would honor the house. I always thought that was a great way for Uncle John to get such a perfect place.

Behind it, attached to it by a long, low shed, sat the barn, built on the leeward side of the slope to protect it from icy winter blasts. Uncle John had converted it into his studio. Even as a child I had envied him that enormous space, overflowing with light. I could gladly have spent the rest of my life there.

Caleb pulled up in front and parked on a level stretch of grass overlooking the water. On this side, too, the rocky shore ran from the top of the slope to the water's edge fifty feet below. Today the waves were swells that broke on the rocks with a high spray of white water that left pools of yellow foam in the curves of the rocks. The schooner was still anchored in the harbor, riding the swells with a dancer's grace.

P.J. immediately headed for the rocks.

"Surf's up today, P.J.," I called. "Be careful."

He paused only long enough to shoot me a look of disdain, then headed down the slope.

Thinking I would give Caleb a minute alone to walk up to the house, I unslung my camera and focused it on the harbor. I snapped two pictures of the schooner, then turned to find Caleb waiting for me, his face tense and strained.

"She reminds me of your father's boat, the *Innisfree*," I said.

"Yes, but she's not. The man who bought her had the hull painted black. And he was going to take her south to the Bahamas." His voice dripped disgust.

As we walked toward the house, I stopped to take a picture of it. Again he waited, so it was easy to back up a couple of steps and casually snap a quick picture of him in front of the house. Even the lighting was right.

All the shutters on the house had been closed and latched to protect the windows against the easterly winter winds. Only the panels on either side of the front door remained uncovered. We pressed our foreheads against the cool glass and peered inside. From where we stood, we could see the long front hall, part of the parlor with its marble fireplace, and, on the other side of the hallway, the library. Behind lay the dining room, kitchen, and a downstairs bedroom and bath that used to be mine when we came to visit.

Caleb stood at the window for several minutes. He tried the front door but found it locked. We walked around the house, where he tried the door to the back entranceway, but it was locked as well. When we came to the shed, though, we were surprised to find the door ajar and went in. The connecting door to the main house was secured, but the passageway into the barn was open, and we headed into it.

I almost expected Uncle John to be there, hunched on his stool in front of his easel, his large planked worktable strewn with brushes, tubes of paint, cans of oil and turpentine, jars of glazes and fixative. After nine years I could still detect the distinct odor of turpentine and linseed oil. I waited to hear his voice and see the smoke rise in soft curls from his pipe. His presence was so strong I had to remind myself he couldn't be there. If I felt like that, I could imagine how Caleb must have been feeling.

He stood in the doorway and took a long, slow look around the barn. "Mr. Bockman was right," he said at last in a quiet voice. "Dad never should have left."

I hesitated, then asked the question Mother would never answer. "Why did he, Caleb?"

"We were pretty broke. Lobstering was bad. Painting was worse. The whole economy here was so bad, paintings were the last things people were buying. If it had just been himself and Mother, I think he would have stayed, but he felt he had me to look out for as well. He didn't want to let me down." A grimace twisted Caleb's face. "So in the end he let us all down — himself most of all."

"Poor Uncle John," I said softly after a moment, searching for a way to change the subject. "I guess he and Evaline had something in common. They both were forced to leave their homes."

"Yeah, except Evaline didn't have a father who could help her out if he had wanted to."

"Wouldn't Grandpa McLaughlin help?"

"Oh, he helped all right," Caleb said bitterly. "He helped by bugging Dad to come to St. Louis and take a job in the business. But he wouldn't loan him the money that might have allowed him to stay here. So in the end Dad had to give in and go. And then, when he got there, Grandfather didn't give him a real job with some responsibility. Dad just sat at a desk and pushed papers all day. It drove him crazy — and no wonder."

"Couldn't Grandpa see what was happening to him?"

"He didn't want to see. Mother and I could see — and we couldn't do a thing about it. But neither one of us ever dreamed he'd kill himself. He kept it all inside."

Caleb turned to me with sudden fierceness. "Sometimes I think this family is cursed — that we *all* carry the burden of it, and we're doomed to repeat it over and over."

Caleb thrust his hands in his pockets and walked away as quickly as he could, through the shed and outside to the Jeep. I couldn't do anything except follow a few paces behind.

Driving away from the house, we were all silent. Blessedly, even P.J. had run out of questions. I was glad, though, that both P.J. and I had come with Caleb. Aunt Phoebe was right. He shouldn't spend too much time alone. Too many dark memories lay in wait for him. I only wished there were something I could do to help bury those memories once and for all.

As we came to a slight rise before heading down into town, I spotted something ahead in the road. Something not too large, but moving. Caleb saw it, too, and slowed the Jeep as we approached. It was a rabbit and it had been hit by a car, but it wasn't dead. Its eyes were open and seemed to be staring at us in fear and pain.

I could see it was the rabbit's hindquarters that had been hit and run over. They lay squashed on the road like a slab of meat with all the bones removed. The rabbit shook its head and twitched its front feet, pawing at the road as if trying somehow to pull itself over to the side, but it couldn't move.

As I watched the rabbit's horrible struggle there in the middle of the road, tears stung my eyes. Behind me, P.J. made a grab for the door handle, but I held the door closed against his efforts.

"Let me out, Molly!" he cried, close to tears. "He's hurt! I want to get him. Let me out!"

I shook my head. "No, P.J.," I said, trying to be firm, but my voice shook. "It's been hurt too bad. It wouldn't even be right to move it. We can't do anything for the rabbit."

"I can try!" he cried, and by now tears were streaming down his face. "Let me try!"

"Molly's right, P.J.," Caleb said, and his voice sounded as if it were a thousand miles away. "We can't save this rabbit."

"Then k-kill it!" P.J. cried out, sobbing so hard he stuttered. "R-run over it again so it doesn't s-suffer any more!"

"Yes, Caleb, please!" I said with urgency myself now. "It's so pitiful. Put the poor thing out of its misery."

Slowly Caleb backed up the Jeep and started forward again, picking up speed.

"Don't look, P.J." was all I had time to say.

But just as we got to the rabbit and were about to hit it, Caleb suddenly stepped hard on the brake. The Jeep skidded to a stop. The rabbit still lay twitching in the road. In the back P.J. was crying loudly, too upset to say anything more.

Caleb put the Jeep into park. I looked over at him. His face was like a death mask, still and white.

"Oh, my God," he said in no more than a whisper. He stretched out his arms in front of him over the top of the wheel and dropped his head forward, pressing his forehead against the backs of his hands. He began to shake, his whole body quivering like some solitary leaf clinging to a tree in the middle of a storm.

For a moment I sat paralyzed. Then instinctively, without thought, I said, "I'll drive home, Caleb."

I climbed out and with shaking legs walked around to the driver's side. As I opened the door, Caleb slid over into the other seat, still trembling but quieter now, less shaken by those convulsive tremors.

I backed up and drove forward slowly, around the rabbit. It was still moving, twitching its front paws in its frantic effort to crawl out of the road.

"No, Molly!" P.J. cried from the back as we cleared the rabbit. "Don't just leave it there. Go back!"

"I can't, P.J.!" I said fiercely.

"You've got to kill it! Don't let it suffer any more! Please, Molly!"

"I can't do it!" I shouted at him. I drew a deep breath to keep from bursting into tears. "Some other car will come along in a minute. . . ." Gripping the wheel, I kept going.

Beside me, Caleb stared straight ahead through the windshield.

I looked over at him, and his eyes turned to meet mine. They were dark with shadows and had the look of someone hunted. I wanted to say something reassuring, but the expression in his eyes stopped me.

"Oh, God," he said softly, "will it ever be over?"

Behind me, P.J. was still crying, but at that moment my concern wasn't for P.J.

I reached over, and this time I took Caleb's hand in mine, holding it tightly. His fingers curved around mine. I held his hand all the way home. It didn't even matter that P.J. was watching.

CHAPTER 12 ∽

B Y THE TIME we got home, P.J. had stopped crying except for an occasional snuffle. As I turned into the drive, I slowly released my fingers and Caleb withdrew his hand. Although his body was still tense, his face was quieter and that hunted look had faded from his eyes.

In the rearview mirror I could see P.J. with his chin buried in his chest, the neck of his T-shirt stretched up over his chin. As my eyes caught his, he glared at me.

"I'm sorry, P.J.," I said in a low voice, turning to face him. "I just couldn't do it."

As I opened the door, Caleb reached over and caught my wrist. "I'm the one who should be saying I'm sorry," he said as much to P.J. as to me. That was all. Then he slid from his seat.

He turned to P.J. "I'm going up to my room for a while, P.J. If you feel like it, you're welcome to come on up." He limped up the path to the house ahead of us.

When Mother saw P.J.'s tearstained face, she knew something had happened. I gave her a quick account without mentioning Caleb. "P.J. wanted to bring it home, and I wouldn't let him," was all I said to explain the tears. Then I escaped up to my bedroom.

I stretched out on my bed, staring at the ceiling. After a few minutes I could hear Caleb's guitar and the sound of low voices. P.J. must have taken him up on his invitation. At that moment, more than anything in the world, I wished I could be up there, too. Somehow it didn't seem fair that P.J. could trail Caleb around, go up to his room, spend all the time he wanted to with him, while he was off-limits for me. I couldn't help but wonder about Caleb's reaction to the rabbit. I wasn't sure which bothered me more — the image of the rabbit struggling in the road or the memory of Caleb, his face buried on his arms, shaking uncontrollably.

Neither recollection was one I wanted to dwell on, and I forced my thoughts ahead to Monday, the Fourth of July. I would be with Caleb all day — and all night. My mind drifted into daydreams of all the possible scenes that might take place, all ending with Caleb taking me in his arms.

*

The following day, Friday, Caleb went fishing with Joel again and then stayed to have supper at the Bockmans, so I barely laid eyes on him. I reminded myself the Fourth was only three days away and used the time to work on my drawing for Caleb.

I drove into town to pick up the film I had dropped off the afternoon before, and when I saw the finished photos, a sudden brainstorm about the drawing flashed in my mind. The more I thought about it, the more excited I became. I sat on the porch and began to do some quick sketches.

With my drawing to keep me occupied, the day and evening passed more quickly than I would have dreamed. As always when I was at work, the world around me faded, and the drawing itself carried me to a place inside myself where everything else seemed dim and unimportant. But this time I found myself looking up now and then, listening for that soft sighing sound I had grown to recognize — or the sound of a woman mourning. But the only sound was the surf breaking on the rocks below.

On Saturday, though, my dream of Monday started to unravel. I awoke to find it pouring, a driving rain straight out of the northeast that looked as if it could go on for days. The thought of bad weather on the Fourth hadn't even occurred to me. What if the carnival and fireworks had to be canceled and Caleb and I were stuck at home with P.J. and Roger all day? The possibility was too depressing to even think about.

Then, over breakfast, Caleb announced that Joel wanted to go with us to the celebration. My heart sank. So much for being alone with Caleb all day.

But that wasn't the worst.

"Joel said he'd get another girl to come along," Caleb went on, "so we'll have a foursome. Kind of a double date."

"That's a wonderful idea!" Mother said with so much enthusiasm I could have strangled her. "As you said, Molly, the more the merrier. Right?"

I couldn't even respond. I just sat and stared at my fried eggs until they were too congealed to eat.

When Mother finally finished her coffee and left the kitchen, I looked up at Caleb and found him watching me. With a quick lift of his eyebrows, he gave an apologetic little shrug.

"Sorry, Molly. I didn't see any way to put him off."

"I know," I replied with a sigh. "That's okay." I took comfort in knowing Caleb seemed disappointed, too. "But is this 'other girl' for Joel or for you?" I asked.

"He didn't specify," Caleb said with a smile that turned up one corner of his mouth. "Judging how often Joel mentions your name, though, my guess is that the 'other girl' is for me."

That was the final blow. Not only would it be agony watching another girl hanging on Caleb all day, but even worse, Joel was considering me his date. The day hadn't even arrived, and already it was falling apart in little pieces.

By Sunday, though, the weather began to clear and the air smelled fresh and moist, full of salt and seaweed, the way it does after a storm. The rocks had collected a whole new selection of treasures, and P.J. and Roger were in bliss exploring and culling. Even Mother took part of the morning off and came down to the beach with sandwiches that we ate sitting on the rocks while the wind blew our hair every which way.

Caleb was relaxed and at ease. Watching his smile appear more readily, catching his eye now and then in response to a shared joke or an offhand remark, made me almost giddy. But while Mother was there I was careful not to look at him too often or stand too close.

Sunday night, after I was in bed and already daydreaming the fantasies that carried me into sleep each night, Mother came into my room.

"Molly, I've been giving careful consideration to leaving you all alone tomorrow," she began in her most lawyer-like voice. I held my breath. "I won't ask Mrs. Pattishaw to stay overnight on one condition."

"What's that?" I asked, fearing some impossible promise she was going to demand.

"I don't think I need to spell it out to you. You know what my concerns are. I just don't want anything to happen that might add to those concerns."

"It won't, Mother. Honestly. I'll be with Joel most of the time, anyway."

"Well, the same goes for Joel, too, you know," she said briskly.

This time I laughed. I could reassure her on that point with no qualms whatsoever.

"Don't worry," I said. "Absolutely nothing's going to happen, Mother. Joel's nice, but that's all. And Caleb's nice. And I'm nice. We're all nice, so there's nothing to worry about." I gave another little laugh and was relieved when Mother smiled in return.

"Okay," she said and leaned over to kiss me good night. "Watch out for P.J. Don't let him get into any mischief, either. I should be able to get back Tuesday night. I'll catch a late ferry, so don't wait supper."

At the door she turned with a little frown of misgiving. "If anything comes up — anything at all — you can reach me at the office, you know, or leave a message. If I'm not there, I'll be at the apartment."

"Sure," I agreed, nodding my head to show her I understood perfectly.

I knew, though, I wouldn't be making any call. I lay back on my bed, giving myself up to my dreams of Caleb. Knowing he was forbidden only made the dreams all the more intense. In that mysterious place deep within that I had never explored, expectation awakened sensations of pleasure I had never felt before — especially not with the boys whose hands had groped for me in the dark on the way home from parties or dances. I found them only a nuisance, but Caleb's hands I would have welcomed. My feelings scared me because they were unfamiliar, but I wanted them never to end.

As I lay there in the dark, my bed, my room, and the whole house rose in the deepening night and dissolved in a mist over roofs and trees, drifting unseen out across the waves. I closed my eyes and gave myself up to those shadowy feelings, diving deep in a dream of my cousin Caleb.

*

When I awoke the next morning, I realized my worry about the weather had been needless. Through the window I could see the sky was bright blue, and a warm breeze was blowing off the ocean. It was a perfect day for the Fourth of July. My hopes began to rise.

While I was dressing, I heard the phone ring and Caleb's voice in the downstairs hall.

"That was Joel," he said with a little frown, looking up at me as I came downstairs. "He offered to pick us up, but I told him we had to drive your mom to the two o'clock ferry and would have a full load. I said we'd meet them at the ferry. Okay?"

"Sure," I agreed. I tried not to sound too elated. That meant we'd be driving home without Joel and the other girl.

"Not disappointed?"

"Hardly!" I said.

Caleb smiled. "Neither am I."

For a minute neither of us moved, and from the expression in his eyes I felt sure he wanted to kiss me. Then Mother's footsteps approached from the kitchen. Caleb turned and walked casually away.

Only five more hours, I thought.

Caleb spent the morning on the veranda with his guitar and sheets of composition paper spread out around him, while I worked upstairs in my room on preliminary sketches for my drawing. I had decided to do it in pen and ink with just a touch of watercolor here and there as highlight.

Before I began with ink, though, I had to draw all the parts lightly in pencil to make sure they were right. This drawing had to be perfect. I thought about going out to the cabin to work, but I enjoyed hearing the snatches of Caleb's music that floated up to my room. Now and then a fragment of melody caught my ear, making me lift my pencil to listen.

Shortly before one-thirty, I changed into a dress my father had sent from Mexico for my birthday. It was white cotton gauze embroidered with bright flowers around the hem and scoop neckline that set off my dark skin and eyes. I hoped Caleb would notice, too. Then Roger arrived, hopscotching up the road, and we all left for Bucks Harbor.

By the time we arrived, the town was already beginning to fill, and it took us a few minutes to find a parking place. With a few last-minute cautionary instructions, Mother headed for the ferry at the end of the pier. I breathed a sigh of relief and turned to P.J. and Roger.

"Now, remember," I said, "we'll meet you here right after the fireworks. So don't forget where we parked."

Before I'd even finished, the two boys were sprinting down the road in the direction of the carnival that had been set up in the town park a block away. Mother had given P.J. enough spending money to keep him busy the rest of the afternoon and evening.

I was just congratulating myself on finally having Caleb

to myself when Joel's voice called from behind us, "Hey, Molly! Caleb! Here we are!"

We both turned to see Joel coming across the street. But that wasn't the worst of it. Clinging to Joel's arm, dressed all in yellow that made her look like an overblown buttercup, was none other than Peggy Ann. I couldn't believe it. She had tracked down Caleb after all, and now we were stuck with her for the rest of the day. I could have cried.

CHAPTER 13 ⟫

As soon as Peggy Ann spotted Caleb, she broke into a grin. "Small world, isn't it?"

Joel looked at her in surprise. "You know Caleb? Why didn't you tell me?"

"I didn't know that was his name. But we kind of met at the Koffee Kup."

"And this is Molly Todd," Joel said, completing the introductions.

"Hi," Peggy Ann said, finally acknowledging me.

Over the trees we could see the top of a circling Ferris wheel. As we started toward it, Peggy Ann took Caleb's arm, claiming him for her own. We couldn't walk down the crowded sidewalk four abreast, so I had no choice but to walk beside Joel.

Joel glanced at me sideways. "I've been looking forward to this all week," he said with a smile.

"I have, too," I responded. That, at least, was no lie.

As we entered the park we could see the carnival was well under way. Booths decorated with flags and red, white, and blue bunting lined the perimeter of the park. The center section had been reserved for the rides.

We began on the carousel, and that was all right because we each had our own horse. And the bumper cars were no real threat, but on the bubble bounce Peggy Ann managed to sit between Joel and Caleb, and she fell against Caleb every time the car swung in a circle.

At the Ferris wheel, where the seats held only two, she took Caleb's hand and led him into one of the little cars. Joel and I followed, climbing in the car behind them. I leaned back, and Joel reached his arm around, half along the back of the seat, half across my shoulders, his fingers resting on the top of my arm.

I couldn't lean forward again without being insulting, so I stayed there and tried not to watch Caleb and Peggy Ann going around, shoulder to shoulder. Instead I kept my eyes focused on the people wandering below. I caught sight of P.J. and Roger at the cotton-candy stand. P.J. had his face buried in a frothy web of pale pink as big as his head.

"Look," Joel said as our car reached the top and hesitated for a moment. "You can see all the way past the harbor to the open sea. I don't think I've ever seen Bucks Harbor from the air before."

"You've never been on a Ferris wheel before?" I asked, surprised.

"Nope. Never had any reason to want to before today. Now I see what I've been missing." He ran his fingers across my arm below the edge of my sleeve, back and forth, lightly brushing the skin and making it tingle. I looked away and prayed the ride would end soon.

I stared out across the treetops to where sky met sea and thought of Evaline. I wondered how often she had stood all alone on the edge of the shore, looking out at the ocean.

Tomorrow, perhaps, when I talked with the Raintrees, I would know more about how she happened to come to our shore. That thought kept my mind occupied until the Ferris wheel began its slow unloading of couples. Ahead of us, Caleb and Peggy Ann climbed out and waited as our car completed the circuit.

As I climbed out of the car after Joel, Caleb winked at me.

"Let's try some of the booths," he said.

"Good idea," I responded before either Joel or Peggy Ann could object, and the four of us made the rounds of all the booths, stopping at each one. Most of them were games of chance, but some were tests of skill. We tried them all, collecting a motley assortment of prizes — pinwheels, wind-up toys, boxes of Cracker Jack, and dime wristwatches that Peggy Ann lined up on her arm in an array of pink, blue, green, and orange plastic bands.

Caleb and Joel won most of the prizes, but I won a monkey-on-a-stick for guessing which shell had the nickel under it and a watch for throwing hoops over plastic stakes. I gave the watch to Peggy Ann, who added it to the collection on her arm.

The last booth was an air-rifle range where to win a prize you had to hit a parade of ducks swimming across the water. A bored-looking man with greasy hair leaned against the side. He had attempted to grow a scraggly beard. I guessed him to be not much older than Caleb and Joel.

Caleb started to walk on by, but Peggy Ann pulled at his arm.

"Oh, look, Caleb, they have teddy bears here. Try and win one, will you?"

"Let Joel try," Caleb said in a quiet voice.

Joel laid a dollar on the counter and picked up the rifle. The man straightened and eyed Peggy Ann and me.

Joel hit seven of the ten ducks, but that only won another pinwheel.

"Come on, Caleb," Peggy Ann urged. "You try now."

Caleb hesitated, his face tightening. Then he gave a little shrug and picked up the air rifle.

He hit every duck, and the man looked at him in disgust. "You in 'Nam?" he asked.

"Yeah," Caleb answered. "Why? Does that disqualify me?"

"No, but that's how I lose all my best prizes — to you damn vets." He looked at Caleb. "How long you over there?"

"Fifteen months."

"Wounded?"

"Yeah," Caleb said shortly, looking uncomfortable. I could tell he wanted to leave, but the man persisted.

"Was 'Nam as bad as they say?"

"Pretty much."

"You get drafted?"

"No."

The man looked at Caleb. "The hell you say. You mean you enlisted? What'd you do a damn-fool thing like that for?"

Caleb stared back at him. "We all have our reasons. I suppose I wouldn't choose to do it again."

"I'd guess not, for Chrissakes. Stupid, friggin' war. If I was to get drafted, I'd think real hard about heading for Nova Scotia."

"Would you?" Caleb said in an even voice that had a decided chill in it. "I guess that would be your choice, then."

"A better friggin' choice than yours, I'd say!"

Caleb stared at the man through narrowed eyes, then turned on his heel and walked away.

"Hey, you didn't pick your prize!" the man called after him.

"Keep it," Caleb said over his shoulder, limping away through the crowd. Joel and I followed, but Peggy Ann hung back. When she caught up with us, she was holding one of the stuffed bears. No one spoke until we came to a refreshment stand.

"I'm starved!" Peggy Ann said, breaking the silence.

We stopped at the stand and loaded up with hot dogs and fries and Cokes and carried them over to a shady spot under a tree near the bandstand. I ate a couple of fries and sipped on my Coke, but a large lump had settled in the bottom of my stomach. This day was not going at all as I had dreamed it would.

While we were eating, a band arrived and set up electric guitars, drums, a keyboard, and four amplifiers. Caleb walked over to talk with one of the guitar players. The man handed Caleb his guitar, and their two heads bent over the instrument. I had all kinds of rivals I hadn't counted on.

"A penny, Molly," Joel said beside me.

"What?" I answered vaguely.

"You know, for your thoughts. You've been real quiet all day — like you're a million miles away."

"Sorry," I said, trying to smile at him. "I guess I was just thinking about what that man said — about going to Nova Scotia."

"I wouldn't blame him," Peggy Ann said, squinting her eyes against the sun. Today her lids were bright blue. "You'd have to be crazy to enlist."

"Not Caleb," I replied tartly, angered by her implication that there must be something wrong with him. "And it must be really hard for soldiers coming back from Vietnam to see all the protests and everything. Especially if you've been wounded — or maybe had your best friend die in your arms!" I ended hotly, close to tears.

Peggy Ann stared at me, her mouth open in surprise.

"I'm sorry," she said. "I didn't mean to be insulting or anything."

"Hey, let's not fight the war today," Joel said quickly, and I took a long drink of Coke.

"I'm going to find the washroom," Peggy Ann said. She stood up and brushed crumbs off her skirt. "You want to come?" she asked with a glance in my direction.

"No thanks," I said shortly, and with a shrug she walked away.

"So, Molly," Joel said. "How about if next time we make it just ourselves? For a date, I mean." He looked at me, clearly hoping for a positive response.

"I guess so," I said halfheartedly. He frowned, and I knew he sensed something was wrong and couldn't figure out what it was. "Sure, I'd like that," I added, forcing a smile.

I couldn't put him off forever and, after all, it wasn't his fault I couldn't get interested in him. Under any other circumstances, I probably would have been flattered and pleased to go out with Joel.

"How about Saturday, then?" he asked, not allowing me time for a change of heart.

"Fine."

"Maybe we could take in a movie. I'll call you Friday, and we can figure something out."

"A movie would be fine," I said. Already I dreaded Saturday night, not because I didn't like Joel but because he wasn't Caleb. At least Mother would be happy.

The band began to play, and Caleb made his way back to our spot under the tree.

"Hey, I almost forgot to tell you," Joel said as Caleb sat beside us and leaned against the tree. "I talked with Dwayne last night, and he says to say hello to you, Caleb." He turned to me. "And a real special hello to you, Molly. He said he remembers you following him around like his shadow and wants to know, would you still fetch things for him like you used to?"

"No way! Not on your life," I said and blushed. "Anyway, I only stuck to him for protection from you two."

"That's not how I remember it," Caleb said with a teasing smile.

I was spared having to respond by a crackle of the amplifiers and blare of drums and electric guitars. The band opened with a rock version of "Stars and Stripes Forever" just as Peggy Ann reappeared.

People began to wander over to the bandstand from the booths and rides, and by the time the song was over a fair-sized crowd had gathered and applauded halfheartedly at the end. The band, evidently deciding one patriotic song was enough for this Fourth of July, swung into a medley of Doors songs, and the crowd's enthusiasm grew. They began with "Break On Through to the Other Side," and several couples moved onto the temporary dance floor that had been set up in the clearing in front of the bandstand.

The music blasted through the amplifiers at a level that

must have carried all the way across the three-mile stretch to New Dover. This band was hardly the Doors, but what they lacked in finesse, they made up in volume. Conversation was impossible, so we sat on the grass and watched the dancers bounce around the floor, each in his or her own space, oblivious of any partner.

When they moved into "Light My Fire," Peggy Ann jumped up and began to swing her hips and shoulders in time to the music. The flounces of her dress rose and fell like yellow waves. She held her hand out to Caleb, an invitation to dance.

"Sorry," Caleb yelled with a rueful smile. "My leg would never make it through this one."

Peggy Ann glanced at Joel, reached down a hand, and pulled him to his feet. Without protest, he followed her onto the dance floor.

Caleb shifted his position against the tree, clearing a space beside him.

"Hey," he said, patting the ground, "you might as well be comfortable."

I moved next to him and leaned against the tree. The western sky was ablaze with the setting sun, but there in the park, under the trees, darkness was beginning to settle. As dusk folded around us, we watched the dancers in silence, our shoulders touching where they came together against the rough bark of the tree. Where Caleb's arm touched mine, I could feel both the warmth of his flesh and the pulsating rhythm of the song as he moved his shoulder in time to the music. Every time the vocalist, voice throbbing with intensity, repeated the refrain, I felt the same ache deep inside me I felt alone in my room at night. I didn't dare look at Caleb.

From "Light My Fire" the medley shifted to "Touch Me." The tempo slowed, much slower than the Doors version, the level of sound muted, and this time when Caleb spoke he didn't have to shout.

"Peggy Ann's heading this way," he said. "Come on, Molly. Help me up. The best defense is an offense."

I scrambled up and reached down a hand to pull Caleb up. Peggy Ann, with Joel behind, appeared from the right just as Caleb and I, hand in hand, veered to the left onto the wooden dance floor.

We came together, face-to-face, in the middle of the floor. Caleb's arm slipped around my waist, and with no hesitation he pulled me to him. Everyone else on the floor was dancing apart, moving slower now to the different beat but still separated. But Caleb, hampered by his leg, held me to him, his right hand pressed against the small of my back, his left hand holding mine, palm against palm.

We moved in a slow two-step across the floor, keeping time with the music but not attempting much beyond that, until we came to the far side, away from the tree where Joel and Peggy Ann were waiting for us to return. My forehead came to rest against Caleb's chin. He smelled of sunshine and soap, the same scent I had caught on his pillow. I inhaled deeply and closed my eyes, relaxing against his chest, feeling the curve of his body against mine. All the earlier disappointments of the day dissolved.

The vocalist began to sing the lyric, but the only line I heard was the one where he begs to be touched, saying he isn't afraid.

For a brief moment Caleb held me away from him, his eyes fastened on mine, a look of longing reflected there, and I was sure he had been listening to the lyric, too. Then his arm tightened around my waist and he pulled me close. Neither of us spoke until the song had ended. It was the last song of the medley, and at the end an unexpected silence fell.

Caleb held me, and we stood together in place. As his body leaned into mine, I closed my eyes, knowing he, too, felt the same yearning I did. Instinctively I pressed against him, moving my body against his, swaying there.

In the silence I heard his voice in my ear. "Molly, Molly, what have you done to me?"

For a brief moment he pulled me even closer. The other couples began to drift away, moving in ones and twos off the floor. I wanted never to move.

After a long moment he took a half step backward, breaking the contact between us.

I lifted my face. He closed his eyes and bent his head to kiss me. At that moment I knew I would do anything for him, anything at all, without regret.

CHAPTER 14 ⟡

T HE REST OF the evening passed in a blur. By the time Caleb and I made our way back to Joel and Peggy Ann, the evening had painted a wash of indigo across the western sky. I wondered if Joel had seen Caleb kissing me and felt a rush of relief when I saw the look of unconcern on his face.

"Maybe we should head for the fireworks and get a front-row seat," Caleb suggested before Peggy Ann could ask him to dance again.

"Good idea," Joel responded with a laugh. "A bunch of little kids like us wouldn't want to miss anything."

We wandered slowly toward the beach at the end of the park. Peggy Ann walked beside Caleb, laughing up at him. I was still floating, lost in my own fantasy, and didn't even care. And when Joel reached over and took my hand, I was hardly aware of it. I let him hold it all the way to the end of the boardwalk.

We leaned against the snow fence that had been erected as a temporary safety barrier and waited for the fireworks to begin. Overhead the indigo was deepening to black, and the first stars gleamed against the dark velvet of the night.

Behind us, in the east, the moon had already begun its rise, an amber globe that hung above the Bucks Harbor rooftops.

The fireworks began as a series of rockets that fanned a shower of colors against the dark sky. The crowd let loose with a chorus of ooohs and aaahs. I glanced around, trying to spot P.J. and Roger in the crowd, hoping they'd found a good place along the fence to watch.

For a town the size of Bucks Harbor, the fireworks were impressive, but before long my thoughts jumped ahead to the time when Joel and Peggy Ann would leave and Caleb and I would start home together. Of course we would have P.J. and Roger with us, but they seemed no more than a minor inconvenience. As soon as we arrived home, I knew they would disappear.

I was startled out of my reverie by the burst of a final rocket that spread a glittering American flag across the sky. The crowd applauded, then gradually began to drift away.

The four of us strolled toward the street where we had parked the Jeep. As we neared the car, I was surprised to see P.J. and Roger already there. One look at P.J.'s face was enough to tell me why he had been so prompt. In the glow of the streetlight, it was a ghostly white. His stomach was clearly rebelling at an overabundance of cotton candy, hot dogs, and too many rides on the bubble bounce. As much as I didn't relish dealing with a sick little brother, I knew an upset stomach would send him right to bed as soon as we got home.

When P.J. spotted us coming down the sidewalk, a look of relief washed over his face. "Gee, Molly," he called, "it took you guys long enough." He climbed into the backseat and Roger was following when Peggy Ann turned to Caleb.

"You guys aren't going home yet, are you?" she asked

with a little laugh. "Hey, the night's still young. What do you say we get a nightcap at the Whale's Belly?" She nodded in the direction of the bar across the street.

"Sure," Joel agreed with a quick smile in my direction. "Why not? The boys can go on some more rides. We won't stay long."

I looked at Caleb.

"Molly's not twenty-one," he said slowly. "Will they let her in?" I was grateful he hadn't said, "Molly's only seventeen."

"Oh, sure," Peggy Ann said, dismissing the problem with a toss of her head. "They're not very strict. I'm only twenty but I can sometimes get served — depending on the bartender. Molly can always get a Coke or something."

"Sure, then why not?" Joel repeated.

"Molly!" P.J.'s voice called from the back of the Jeep with urgency. "I gotta go home, Molly!"

I looked at him and knew he meant it. By this time his face was tinged with green and he looked miserable. I had to get him home before he was sick right there in the street.

Reluctantly I turned to the others. "You all go. I've got to take P.J. home. He's not feeling so good."

"I'll go with you, then," Joel said quickly. "We can go in my car, and Caleb and Peggy Ann can stay here and bring the Jeep whenever they want."

My stomach dropped into my shoes. The last thing I wanted was for Joel to drive me home to an empty house. Even worse was the thought that P.J. might get sick in his car. Peggy Ann still held Caleb's arm, and he wouldn't look at me.

"Molly, let's go home!" P.J. said plaintively. I knew he was close to tears.

"No, that's okay, Joel," I said quickly and started to climb into the driver's seat. "I don't want to spoil everybody's fun. You three go ahead. I'll take the boys home."

I reached out my hand for the keys, and Caleb handed them to me without a word. I didn't dare look at him.

"I wish you'd let me go with you, Molly," Joel said as I started the engine. "Are you sure you'll be okay?"

"Of course I'll be okay!" I said with more vehemence than I intended. "It's only a few miles."

Before he could protest further, I pulled out of the parking space and headed down the street. In the rearview mirror I could see the three of them crossing the street to Whale's Belly.

Halfway home, P.J. said with sudden urgency, "I don't feel so good, Molly. You better stop."

I pulled off the road and opened the door. When P.J. was barely out of the car, he bent double and was sick in the grass beside the road.

The odor made me gag, but I held his head, and when everything had come up, I found a rumpled tissue to wipe his perspiring face.

"I'm sorry, Molly," he said in a pitiful voice. "I didn't mean to spoil your fun."

I gave him a quick squeeze. "That's okay, P.J. I didn't really want to go with them, anyway. We can both get a good night's sleep."

By the time we got home, P.J. was dozing in the back. After dropping Roger off at his house, I helped a drowsy P.J. inside and up to bed.

"Thanks, Molly," he mumbled just before he drifted off. "For a sister, you're okay."

"That's what sisters are for, pal. Someday it'll be the other way around."

I tiptoed out through our connecting bathroom into my room, leaving both doors open in case he was sick again. I got out my sketch pad and began to draw, waiting for the sound of Joel's car in the drive that would signal Caleb's return. My mind wouldn't focus on the drawing, and when I looked at the pad a few minutes later, I discovered I had drawn only a series of pointless doodles. With a sigh, I set the pad aside.

A few minutes later, I went in to check on P.J. and found him sleeping soundly. I wandered downstairs, got a can of cold beer, and went out to sit on the porch steps, telling myself that if they could all go to the bar, I could certainly have one lousy beer all by myself at home. I sipped half-heartedly at the beer, not really enjoying it but making myself drink it until the can was almost empty.

The beer only made me sleepy. I yawned and looked at my watch. It was almost midnight, and I knew Caleb was planning to fish with Joel tomorrow and wouldn't want to get to bed too late. I decided to wait another half hour and if he wasn't home by then, I'd give up waiting and go to bed. For all I knew, he might be having a wonderful time with Peggy Ann.

The longer I sat on the steps, the sleepier I got — and the more depressed. The one night Mother was away, the one night I had a chance to be alone with Caleb, and this was all it had come to — sitting by myself on the porch steps drinking a beer I didn't even like. The only thing that brightened the dismal night was the thought that tomorrow the Raintrees would be home. Tomorrow maybe I would get one step closer to solving the mystery of Evaline Bloodsworth.

I stared at the ocean, thinking of the mariner alone on the sea in his ghost ship with no one to talk to or share his suffering. And all because of the thoughtless act of killing the albatross. The thought made me shiver, and I almost wished Evaline would appear again. Tonight I could have used a friend, even a silent, shadowy one.

Overhead, the sky was alight with stars and the reflected light of the moon. The sound of the waves breaking high on the rocks told me the tide was full. With a sigh that started in my toes and moved all the way up to the lump in my throat, I set down my empty beer can and walked down the drive and across the road. At the edge of the incline I watched the white water sweep across the black rocks. Usually the rhythm of the waves soothed me, but tonight the sound made me feel lonely. The longer I stood there, the more dejected I grew. I felt a little giddy from the beer and realized it was only making me sadder.

The more melancholy I became, the angrier I grew, until finally the anger displaced the sadness. What was the matter with Caleb, anyway? Why didn't he make Joel and Peggy Ann bring him home? He must know I'd be waiting up for him — our one chance to be alone together. And not only that, he had ruined tomorrow by agreeing to go fishing with Joel. He must have done it all on purpose. Knowing how much I wanted him to come home, he was deliberately staying away. It struck me, then, that perhaps he was staying away because he didn't trust himself to be alone with me. But even this thought didn't lift my deep gloom.

I picked up a stone and heaved it into the ocean, where it was swallowed by a dark wave. Well, I thought, if that's the way he wants to be, to hell with him. I turned on my heel and started back to the house.

Before I had even crossed the road, I heard it. The muffled sound of a woman crying, the same crying I had heard the night of Caleb's arrival. But this time it was softer, as though the woman had been crying so long that by now she was worn out, exhausted by her grief. I stopped in my tracks and held my breath, afraid to move, terrified because of the darkness and the fact that I was alone. Encountering the young girl Evaline in daylight or in the sanctuary of my bedroom was one thing, but this was something else again. And although I connected the crying with Evaline, I couldn't be sure it was she.

Without moving, I took a quick look up and down the road but saw nothing. I waited, shivering even though the night was warm. The crying died away. I realized I had been holding my breath and took a deep inhalation of air as I ran across the road and up the drive. Then I heard it again, a soft keening now, almost like the whimper of a young animal in search of its mother, and this time I knew the sound came from directly ahead of me. I came to an abrupt stop in the driveway and peered through the darkness.

She was there on the veranda in the rocker, moving slowly forward and back, hidden in the shadows. I knew immediately the figure was a woman, but it was not the young girl Evaline. I covered my mouth with my hand to hold back a scream.

The woman was hunched over, her face buried in her hands, her body swaying in time to her low keening. Then she raised her head, and I could see her more clearly. Even in the shadows I could tell this woman was old, older than Mr. Bockman or my own grandmother, and when she raised her head her long, white hair tumbled across her stooped shoulders.

It was the old woman Caleb had seen on the beach the day he arrived, the old woman Mr. Bockman said had been sighted now and then wandering along this stretch of shore. Evaline as she must have looked just before she died. Because she sat in the shadow of the porch, I could only see her eyes, large and dark, staring at me across the distance that separated us. Her eyes drew me forward, one slow step at a time, until I stood a few feet from the bottom of the steps.

"Why are you here?" I whispered at last.

She began to moan again, a soft cry that was barely audible, but the sound of it was so bereft, so full of despair, that I felt my own eyes fill with tears.

"What do you want me to do?" I whispered.

Slowly she raised her hand and stretched it forward, holding it out to me. She wanted me to take her hand. A rush of fear swept over me, and I couldn't move. I was terrified that if she took my hand I might get pulled into some unseen world with her and never find my way back. I stood rooted.

She rose from the chair and moved toward me out of the shadow of the veranda. I was frozen, unable to run or even take a step. For the first time I could see she had form and substance, and yet at the same time she was not quite solid. She moved down the steps in the same way the girl Evaline had crossed my room, as though her feet were not quite touching the floor.

Shadowed now by the old pine that hid the light of the rising moon, the old woman stood facing me. She reached out her hand toward my face, and I finally stepped backward, terrified of her touch. But her finger touched my cheek, a touch so light I barely felt it.

"What is it?" I asked, my voice a faint rasp.

She looked at me and slowly shook her head back and forth, like a warning. In her eyes I saw an expression of such sadness it made my heart contract. It took my breath away because I suddenly sensed the sadness was not for herself, like her crying. This time it was for me.

My legs began to tremble, and I reached for the post at the bottom of the steps, holding onto it for support. Slowly the old woman turned and moved away, down the front lawn, across the road, and beyond the ridge of the rocky slope until she disappeared from view.

Still trembling, I made my way upstairs, undressed, and fell into bed. I closed my eyes and tried to sort out what had happened, but none of it made any sense. Somehow, though, I knew I had failed her. My fear had stood in the way of discovering the reason she had come — just as my fear had kept me from following Caleb his first night on the island.

I lay in bed, remembering the look of sadness in her eyes, wondering what she was seeking. The one comforting thought was that by that time tomorrow I might be closer to an answer.

My last thought before I finally fell asleep was one of surprise. Seeing Evaline had, for a while, made me forget everything else — even the fact that I had been waiting for Caleb to come home. I let sleep overtake me, too drained even to care any longer.

CHAPTER 15 ∽

AFTER JUST A short sleep I awakened with a start to the sound of cries, someone calling from a distance. I lay flat on my back, listening, my heart racing. At first I thought it was the same crying I had heard earlier that night. But gradually I realized it wasn't a woman's voice at all but a man's, and the cries weren't coming from outside but from above my room where Caleb was sleeping.

Throwing on a bathrobe over my pajamas, I flicked on the light in the hallway and started upstairs, my legs shaking. This time, I told myself, I won't back away.

Halfway up, I heard him call out in a muffled voice, "Don't do it! Don't fire! Oh, God, don't fire!"

He was calling out in a dream. I ran the rest of the way up and crossed the room to the side of his bed. The light from the hallway cut a swath up the stairwell, and the moonlight, too, spilled through the unshaded window, filling the room with a wash of pale light. Caleb was tossing restlessly on the bed. I didn't want to startle him awake by turning on a light.

He was wearing pajama bottoms but no top. The sheet had twisted around his legs, and he was kicking and thrashing in an attempt to get free. In the pale light his face shone with sweat, and when I touched his forehead my fingers came away wet.

"I can't! Don't make me!" he cried out again, but this time the words were deep in his throat, almost a sob.

I sat beside him and shook his shoulder gently.

"Caleb, wake up," I said softly, but his eyes stayed closed. His head tossed back and forth on the pillow. For the first time since Mother had left, I suddenly wished she were there. I leaned closer and shook him harder. "Caleb, wake up! You're dreaming, Caleb. Wake up!"

His eyes flew open, and with a sudden thrust that almost knocked me off the bed, he abruptly sat upright. "What is it?" he cried out. "What's happened to them?"

"Caleb, you're dreaming," I said again, gripping his shoulder, frightened by the intensity of the nightmare he couldn't seem to throw off. "You're having a nightmare. It's me, Caleb. Molly. I'm here with you." My voice shook. "Caleb, it's all right now. It's all right." I said it over and over until at last he drew a deep, shuddering breath and turned to me.

"Molly?" I could see his eyes now, gleaming darkly in the dim light. "Oh, God, it was that dream again, wasn't it?"

"You were having a nightmare," I said, relieved that at least he was awake and recognized me, but I didn't let go of his shoulder.

"Yes, I know," he said at last, and I could feel him shiver. "I used to have it a lot. But it hasn't come for a while now. I thought maybe it had stopped."

"It's okay, it's okay," I whispered. My fingers moved across his back, rubbing the skin of his shoulders and neck.

He leaned forward, resting his forehead on his drawn-up knees, and for a moment I hesitated.

"Don't stop," he said.

"Do you want the light on?" I asked, continuing to knead his taut muscles.

He shook his head, and I rubbed his back in silence, aware of the feel of his flesh, the dampness of his skin, the firm muscles of his shoulders and back. I remembered that first morning when I had rubbed lotion into his back. It seemed like a lifetime ago.

With a sudden motion he swung his legs over the side of the bed and stood up, surprising me. He crossed to the bureau and opened the little leather-lined box I had invaded just a week ago. He lifted out the pack of cigarettes, but it was the letter I thought of, that letter lying at the bottom of the box.

He took a cigarette and lit it, inhaling deeply twice. "Do you want one?" he asked and I shook my head. "You're smart not to have started. I used to smoke like a chimney, but the doctors told me in no uncertain terms I'd better quit. I pretty much have — except for times like this."

He came back and sat beside me on the bed. "Did I say anything?" he asked after a moment. "While I was dreaming, I mean."

"You kept saying 'Don't do it, don't fire.' And then you said, 'Don't make me.' You scared me, Caleb. You sounded so sad, so . . . so . . ." I groped for the right word that would describe what I had heard. "So tormented," I said at last in a whisper.

"That's what the nurses in the hospital said, too," he replied in a flat voice. He leaned back against the headboard and inhaled again deeply.

"Were you dreaming about Vietnam?" I asked.

"Yeah," he said again, exhaling a long trail of smoke that

drifted around us. Flicking the ashes into the ashtray beside him, he stretched his legs down the length of the bed and closed his eyes.

I thought of Mother's warning not to ask Caleb questions about Vietnam. But P.J.'s questions hadn't seemed to bother him. And something about the hour or the softness of the moonlight or the fact that we were alone and sitting together on his bed made me not worry about it.

"What happened over there that you dream about?" I asked at last.

"Different things that get all mixed up together."

"Maybe it would help to talk about them."

He stared at the glowing end of the cigarette between his fingers and was silent so long I thought he was going to ignore my suggestion.

"You told me your nightmare," he said at last. "I suppose it's only right that I tell you mine."

"Only if you want to," I replied, suddenly worried that I had pushed too hard.

"It's not very nice."

"Nightmares are never very nice," I said and waited as he took another drag. He held the smoke in his lungs a moment, then exhaled slowly with his eyes still closed.

"I meant *I* wasn't very nice. What happened — what I dream about — isn't something I'm proud of. In fact, I try hard *not* to think about it, but every now and then, like tonight, it comes crawling out to remind me."

"Remind you of what, Caleb?" I asked, tentatively.

"Of what fighting in a war can make us do sometimes." He opened his eyes and looked at me a long time. "I never told you how lovely you looked today, Molly."

Surprised, I let my eyes fasten on his, and they held me.

"I'd hate for you of all people to think badly of me," he went on.

"I couldn't," I whispered. "Not ever. No matter what you might have done."

He held out his hand to me, and I took it, so aware of his touch and the feel of his fingers moving against mine that at first, as he started to talk, I barely heard what he was saying.

"In the dream, a lot of things get all jumbled up," he began slowly. He closed his eyes again, his head still resting against the headboard. "Another forward observer and I were sent ahead to scout out a Vietcong position and send back the coordinates. We were told the place had been the base for a lot of ambushes. The captain said it was a free-fire zone — an area that's considered enemy territory whether or not the people in it are known to be hostile."

I waited as he took another drag, then watched the smoke as he exhaled slowly.

"We moved ahead to where this position was supposed to be, but all we found was a group of huts that looked like an ordinary native village. I wanted to see what was going on before we sent back the position, so we waited and we watched. We didn't see anything except villagers walking around. Natives — women and kids mostly, some old people and a few animals. That was about it." He flicked the cigarette against the ashtray.

"So the other guy — his name was Carl — calls in and tells the captain we don't see any VC, just villagers. The captain says again it's a free-fire zone and never mind making judgments, just do the job. He tells us if we don't send the right position, he'll have us up for court-martial."

Caleb stared again at the glowing end of the cigarette as

if it held the rest of the story. Then he went on more slowly.

"So Carl phoned in the coordinates, and they began shelling. A barrage. Some of the shells were incendiaries. And all the while Carl and I were watching through the binoculars. And what we saw . . . that's what I still see. That's what comes back in the nightmare."

Caleb opened his eyes and looked at my hand, studying my palm and tracing the lines with his finger as though they held the past. I wasn't sure if he'd go on. I wasn't even sure I wanted to hear it.

Running his finger back and forth across my palm, he started to talk again, staring at my hand as though the pictures in his mind were etched on its surface.

"That was when I quit looking, but by then we could smell the burning flesh. It's a smell I still can't get rid of. Sometimes I wake in the middle of the night with it still in my nostrils."

He paused, rolling the stub of the cigarette between his fingers, around and around. After a minute he went on, but his voice was so low I had to bend forward to catch it.

"We'll never know, Carl and I, if that was the camp that had been ambushing us or if it was just a village trying to exist. We'll never know because there was no one left alive to tell us, just like I'll never know about my father and what might have happened if I had gone home on the bus that day."

He opened his eyes and stared at the ceiling, and I wondered if he was seeing the people in that village or his father slumped over the wheel. I searched for something to say, knowing that whatever I said couldn't make a difference. No words could wipe away those images that kept coming back to him in his dreams.

"You can't blame yourself, Caleb," I said at last in as strong a voice as I could summon. "Not about your father or the people in the village either. Those weren't your choices. And the village would have been destroyed sooner or later, anyway, even if you hadn't done it. And maybe the captain was right — I mean about the village being the place doing the ambushing."

"Yeah," Caleb said again in that flat voice that scared me more than the tight line of his mouth. "That's what the shrink said, too. And the funny thing is, in my head I know it's true. But knowing that doesn't make the dream go away. Except my dream is all mixed up with something else."

He gave a sudden shudder that shook his whole body and took another long inhalation on what was left of the cigarette. I looked at his eyes. In the dim light his pupils were dilated, two black circles swimming in a sea of green.

"What else, Caleb?" I asked after a moment. "What else happened?" Hearing his story only made me feel more connected to him. I knew that telling a nightmare somehow softens it, makes it no less vivid but less harsh. I remembered my dream about searching for my baby in the hospital and the terrible sense of emptiness and loss I had felt. Telling the dream to Caleb hadn't changed it or made me forget it, but the feeling had been more bearable.

He looked at me and shook his head. "Nothing," he said in the same flat voice. He took a last deep drag on the cigarette, then stubbed it out into the ashtray and leaned his head back again. As he exhaled a long plume of smoke and watched it float upward, his eyes closed to narrow slits as though he were peering at something from a great distance. "Nothing I can talk about."

His face had that closed, guarded look I had seen when he first came to the island.

"Wouldn't it be better if you did talk about it?" I asked. "That's what you said about your father. Remember? You said he kept everything inside so no one could help him. Don't do that, Caleb. Please."

"You don't want to hear it, Molly."

"Yes, I do. I want to hear whatever concerns you, whatever's giving you those nightmares. I want them to go away. I care about you, Caleb!"

I wanted to lie down beside him, wrap my arms around him, and hold him until everything hurtful in his life faded away. But I sat where I was on the edge of the bed, afraid that if I moved any closer he would back away. He didn't look at me but stared at the ceiling.

"I've never told anyone this, Molly," he said, "not even the shrink. I don't know if I can tell it now, even to you."

"Try, Caleb," I whispered. "Please just try."

Whether it was the lateness of the hour and the effect of the moonlight or simply because he had kept it all inside so long, he began the rest of the story in a halting voice.

"It was the night of the ambush," he said, still staring at the ceiling. "The night we crossed the mine field, the night I was wounded." He stopped, as though searching for words that had been bottled up too long. "One of the first mines that detonated wasn't far from me. I looked over and could see someone had been hit. Then, in the light of a flare, I saw who it was."

Caleb's voice was shaking, and he stopped and drew a deep breath. I could guess what was coming, and I dreaded hearing it.

"His name was Robert Englehart."

The name left a great weight in the pit of my stomach, but I sat very still, careful not to give any sign of recognition.

Caleb took another deep breath. "We all called him Bob the Gimp because he was always stumbling over tree roots. We had been together ever since boot camp, and he was my best friend . . . probably the best friend I'll ever have. We had made a pact, a promise, that if either of us was wounded past hope, the other would . . . end it for him. I never dreamed . . ."

His voice trailed off, and he blinked twice, as though trying to clear his vision. He cleared his throat and went on.

"When I got to him, I could see right away it was bad. He must have been right on top of that mine when it exploded. Oh, God, Molly, you can't imagine what he looked like!" Caleb's mouth was a thin line, as though he, too, were feeling the pain of that wound.

"Tell me, Caleb," I whispered so softly I wasn't sure he could even hear me.

"His legs were gone," he said after a moment, and his voice was shaking. "Both of them. All the way up to his hips. Nothing was left but bloody stumps. And above them, a mass of wounds where the mine fragments had torn into him. He had nothing left but his torso. He was . . . emasculated. But the worst of it was that he wasn't dead yet.

"And he was conscious. That was the horrible part. When I got to him, his eyes were wide open and he was looking down at . . . at what was left of him. He was in shock, but he could see what had happened to him . . . and he was beginning to feel pain. It wasn't unbearable yet, but it was only a matter of time."

Caleb's face was tight with the hurt of remembering, and it hurt me, too, to see him that way. I almost reached over to stop him, but he began again. His voice was steadier but flat, almost without expression.

"Bob grabbed my arm and tried to grab my rifle, too. He wanted to shoot himself but didn't have the strength to hold it. He said he couldn't stand staying alive. He begged me to shoot him, pleaded with me."

" 'We made a pact,' he said, 'and I'd do it for you.' He kept saying this over and over. 'You promised, and I'd do it for you if you were like this. I'd do it for you.' And every time a flare went off, I'd see that bloody mess that was only half a person. I looked at him, and I knew he was right. If it had been me, I would have begged him to shoot me, too. I would have begged him until he did it."

Caleb's voice dropped to a whisper. "So finally, I . . . I did what he wanted me to do. Right after that I was shot in the leg. That was when I carried out the three wounded men. And later they gave me the Silver Star. I saved three men I didn't even know, but I couldn't save the one who mattered most to me."

"But it was the only thing you could do, Caleb," I whispered at last in the long silence. "The only thing."

Caleb lay on the bed without moving, his face paper white in the moonlight, his eyes closed. Then very deliberately he stood up and walked to the bathroom, closing the door behind him and turning on the light. A few seconds later, I could hear him being sick. I sat rooted to the bed, knowing there was nothing I could do. The last thing he'd want would be for me to hold his head as I had for P.J. earlier that evening.

So I sat on the bed and waited for him to come out, too

numb to think or even cry. Tears wouldn't come, only that terrible ache at the thought he had killed his best friend in an act of mercy. I thought of the letter lying in the bottom of that box and how Caleb had made sure Robert's mother would never know the agony of her son's death. But I could never say anything about his act of kindness. Not without telling him I had read the letter.

The water in the bathroom splashed into the sink. It ran for a long time, and when Caleb finally came out, his face and hair were wet.

He walked to the window and stood looking out. Outside the waves were beating against the rocks in their endless rhythm. In the path of the moonlight, Caleb stood quietly, but his face was still very pale. Then he turned from the window to face me.

"Poor Molly," he said, and the trace of a smile curved his upper lip. "What we don't do to you. A couple of real invalids. First P.J. and now me. You've had more than your share."

He came back to the bed and stretched out again, face up, his head resting in the palms of his hands. Anything I might have said to him, he would already have told himself a thousand times. So I spoke the only words I knew to say.

"I love you, Caleb," I said. "I guess you know that."

He looked at me a long time, and when he finally answered, his voice was very quiet.

"I don't know of anything I'd have rather heard tonight," he said. Then he smiled at me. "Look at us, Molly. Alone together on my bed in the middle of the night. Wouldn't Aunt Libby have a stroke if she could see us now?" He glanced at the clock on the table whose luminous numbers read 2:30. "In less than two hours, Joel will be by to pick me up."

"Will you be able to get some sleep?" I asked him.

"Yes," he said. "And without the nightmares, I think."

I looked at him, not even weighing what I was about to say.

"I'll stay with you, Caleb. I'll stay the rest of the night. If you'll let me."

He looked back at me. His eyes gleamed in the pale light, his pupils still large.

He reached out his hand and slowly pulled me toward him. I stretched out beside him, my whole body trembling in response to his touch.

His arm reached around me, pulling me to him. For a brief second I saw his face above mine, his eyes searching. I shut my eyes as his mouth closed on mine. His tongue touched my lips and I opened them, welcoming it. He held me tighter, his tongue moving back and forth over mine until I felt as though my flesh and bones were melting.

He reached down and loosened the belt holding my bathrobe. As it fell open, his hands reached inside under the thin fabric of my pajamas. I felt faint with the knowledge that nothing in my fantasies had prepared me for the pleasure that his hands on my body could bring. As though responding to my desire, he shifted me under him as I pressed upward. He raised his head above me, his eyes gleaming, his pupils still large and black.

He looked down at me, his eyes searching my face with a questioning look. "Molly, have you ever . . . ?"

For the briefest second I thought about lying but realized he would quickly learn the truth. I thought of how I had already betrayed his trust once and knew I couldn't play that kind of trick on him.

Slowly I shook my head no.

He leaned above me on one elbow, and I waited, sick with the realization that no matter what he was feeling, he wouldn't allow himself to be the first. He paused, then slowly rolled to one side, and I heard a deep sigh.

"I want it to be you, Caleb," I whispered, aware only of the ache that still throbbed.

"Oh, my God, Molly," he cried, his voice full of anguish. "Don't make this harder than it is!"

"But why won't you? . . . if I want you to . . ."

"Because I've committed enough sins. I won't have you on my conscience, too. My God, Molly, you could almost be my sister!"

He turned to look at me, his eyes sad. "As much as I might want to . . . we both know it would be wrong, and sooner or later it would come back to haunt us. We can't escape what we do, the choices we make." His voice was husky.

I couldn't talk beyond the lump in my throat.

Caleb rubbed his hand across his eyes. "You'd better go, Molly," he said in a tired voice. "Don't tempt me to do something I'll regret."

His words hit me like a slap of his hand. It wasn't just that I hadn't helped him. I had made things more difficult for him because of my own selfish desires.

I stood up and slowly walked to the top of the stairs. I thought once more of begging him to let me stay, but it would have been a cruel thing to do. And I knew he would refuse.

As I started down the steps, I heard him say the words

he had said at the Koffee Kup. "You're my protector, Molly. My guardian angel."

It wasn't until I reached my own room that I realized I had completely forgotten to mention my encounter with the old woman on the porch — my encounter with Evaline. That, too, would have to wait for another time. With a sigh, I crawled into my own bed, sliding between sheets that were cold and empty.

CHAPTER 16

I AWOKE TIRED and drained, with puffy lids and dark circles under my eyes. I hadn't heard Caleb leave to go fishing with Joel.

A long day loomed ahead, and my mind kept drifting to Caleb and the events of the previous night. I was glad to have Evaline to think about and help keep my mind off Caleb and the disappointment that still ached inside of me.

I was eager to call the Raintrees, but the housekeeper had said they wouldn't be home until late in the day. I had to settle for being patient a few more hours and remind myself that before the end of the day I might know more of Evaline's story.

P.J. slept late and awoke with no apparent ill effects of the carnival. I envied his cheerful, rested face with no dark smudges under his eyes. After breakfast we picked up Roger and drove down to Windhover, where I shopped for groceries and picked up some enlargements of my photos. I had asked for eight-by-ten glossies of six of the pictures. They cost a bundle, but the results made it worth the expense.

I had perfect pictures of not only Caleb but also his old house and the schooner moored in the harbor. I also had managed to get some good general shots of the waves breaking on the rocks and a gull perched on one leg on a piling at the wharf. Knowing I could use them all in my drawing excited me, and I was anxious to get back home to work on it. I glanced at my watch and saw I had another twenty minutes before meeting the boys back at the car, so I sat on a bench and went through the pile of photos again, examining each one carefully.

Looking at the photo of Caleb brought back all the memories of the night before. I thought of how it might have ended and closed my eyes, longing for what never could be simply because our blood ties were too close. But as much as I knew it was true, I still didn't want to accept it.

"Snatching a little sun or a little nap, Miss Molly?"

I was startled out of my reverie by a gravelly voice I immediately recognized.

"A little bit of both, I guess," I said with a smile, opening my eyes to see Mr. Bockman's sturdy form in front of me.

"Ayuh, I had a hunch. You waiting here for the boys to come in?" he asked with a broad grin. "If so, you got a long wait, young lady."

"Not those boys," I said. "The little ones. My brother, P.J., and his friend. I have to meet them in a few minutes, so I'm glad you came along. The sun feels so good I might have fallen asleep."

"Burning the candle at both ends last night, were you? The missus and me could see the fireworks all the way across the island. It must have been some celebration."

"Oh, it was!" I agreed with what I hoped was the right degree of enthusiasm.

"And how's your star boarder doing? Evaline, I mean, not Caleb. Any sign of her lately?"

"I don't know," I said, dodging the question. "But I might learn something more about her later today. Maybe even about how she came here. I found some descendants of the family she stayed with when she worked in the mill in Lowell."

"Was she in Lowell?"

"Her family sent her there to work in a cotton mill when she was only twelve," I said, without explaining how I knew it.

"I guess I never heard that. Let me know if you find out anything more. Ever since you mentioned her name, you got me thinking about her."

"Me, too, Mr. Bockman. I've got my fingers crossed that these people have some information. I'll let you know."

"You can always send word with Joel." He gave me a quizzical look from under bushy eyebrows. "The way I hear it, you might be seeing a fair amount of him."

"I'll be seeing him this Saturday night," I conceded, trying to smile.

"I had a hunch he might get around to that." His grin stretched a little farther. "The boy shows real good sense. I have to say I envy him."

"Thank you, Mr. Bockman. We're just going to the movies. You're more than welcome to come along, you know," I said with a laugh, thinking it wasn't such a bad idea.

"Somehow I don't think Joel would appreciate that," Mr. Bockman said with a chuckle. "But you have a real good time." He tipped his seaman's cap to me and started away with a little wave of his hand. "Nice seeing you again," he said. "And don't forget to let me know what you learn about poor old Evaline."

I watched him lumber down the sidewalk and around the

corner and then headed back to the Jeep to meet the boys and drive home.

*

I spent most of the afternoon on the veranda, working on the drawing. After my encounter with Evaline the night before, I didn't feel like working in the cabin by myself, and I wanted to be at the house when Caleb got home. As soon as he arrived, I planned to call the Raintrees.

With the photos to work from, getting the drawings right was much easier. I finished all the preliminary sketches and was planning how they should be laid out in the final drawing when Joel's car turned into the drive. I quickly put the sketches in my portfolio and set it in the closet in the front hall. By the time I stepped back out on the porch, Caleb was walking up the path to the house with Joel beside him. I could tell what was coming, and disappointment settled like a stone in the pit of my stomach. I steeled myself to look welcoming.

"Can we feed an extra mouth at supper?" Caleb called. "A hungry one?" Although his voice sounded upbeat, he looked worn out, and his eyes were shadowed by the same dark circles I had seen under my own eyes.

"Sure," I said, trying to sound cheerful, "if you'll settle for spaghetti." I considered it my specialty, and the sauce had been simmering on the stove all afternoon.

"Great," Joel said as we walked inside. "In fact, if that's what I'm smelling now, you couldn't haul me out of here with a steam shovel."

I thought of the Raintrees. As anxious as I was for news of Evaline, I didn't want to call while Joel was there. I wanted to keep Evaline between Caleb and me.

"Caleb offered me the use of his shower, too, if that's

okay," Joel said. "I wouldn't want to ruin a good spaghetti dinner with the smell of fish."

"We're both pretty pungent," Caleb said with a smile. "I'll show you where it is, Joel, and you can go first. Then I think it's time for a beer."

"You're on!" Joel said, taking the steps two at a time as Caleb followed more slowly. His right leg dragged as it always did when he was tired.

As they disappeared upstairs, the phone rang. It was Mother calling from New York.

"I'm at the airport, Molly," she said very fast and somewhat out of breath. "My plane to Bangor leaves in a few minutes, so I shouldn't have any trouble making the nine o'clock ferry. Her words suddenly slowed, as though she were feeling her way. "How's everything been going?"

"Just fine, Mother."

"No problems?"

"No problems at all, unless you count P.J. getting sick last night from too much junk food."

"Oh, well, if that's all . . . I'm glad everything's all right. I tried calling last night and no one answered."

"We didn't get home from the fireworks until after ten."

"That's what I figured and went to bed. If there had been a problem, I assumed you'd call."

"Yes, Mother, I would have called." I twisted a strand of hair around my finger and shifted from one foot to the other, anxious to change the subject.

"Well, I've got to run now, Molly. They're calling my flight. See you tonight. Nine-thirty at the ferry." The line went dead.

I was in the kitchen boiling spaghetti when a sweaty P.J.

burst in the back door followed by an equally sweaty Roger.

"Great! Spaghetti!" he exclaimed, peering in the pot. "Can Roger stay for supper?"

Roger hung in the doorway, grinning sheepishly, clearly hoping an invitation would be extended.

"What the heck," I said. "Joel's here, too. What's one more mouth?"

"Neat!" P.J. responded. "It's a party!" He disappeared into the front of the house, followed by Roger, who tripped over his shoelace on his way through and looked at me with another sheepish grin.

During supper Caleb said little and wouldn't meet my eyes, but his silence was more than filled by the two boys and Joel. P.J. and Roger took advantage of Mother's absence by noisily sucking up their spaghetti, spouting bad knock-knock jokes, and generally being both messy and noisy. I didn't have the heart to stop them. When they were too busy eating to tell their bad jokes, Joel took up the slack with fish stories — most of which sounded like very tall tales but kept us all laughing.

After supper Caleb sent P.J. upstairs for his guitar, and they worked together in the kitchen while Joel and I did the dishes and Roger looked at P.J. in openmouthed admiration. Even I was impressed by P.J.'s progress and made a mental note to urge Mother to get him a decent guitar for his birthday in September. Then Caleb played and sang for us, and all the feelings I had tried so hard to keep buried all evening flooded over me.

Just before nine, Caleb yawned and stretched. The circles under his eyes had deepened. He was almost nodding over his guitar.

"Sorry, folks," he said with an apologetic smile. "I'm going to call it a night. Another five minutes, and I'll be asleep at the table."

"Yeah, me too," Joel said, standing up as if on cue. "I'd better get myself home. Four A.M. comes awful early. Want to go along tomorrow, Caleb?"

"Thanks, I think I'll take a pass and sleep in," Caleb said. I felt a rush of relief.

I turned to find Roger yawning as well. "I'll drop you home on my way to the ferry," I said to him.

"I'll take you, Molly," Joel offered.

Caleb paused in the doorway.

"Absolutely not," I said to Joel, smiling to take the sting out of my second refusal in two days to let him drive me. "It would be at least another hour before you'd get to bed. I'm not going to be responsible for having you fall overboard tomorrow."

"Then I can at least take Roger," he said. "It's on my way. Come on, buddy. You can tell me another knock-knock joke."

Before they were even out the door, P.J. had started up the stairs. A moment later I heard his bedroom door close.

Halfway out the front door, Joel suddenly turned back. "I'll see you Saturday, Molly?"

I nodded, and he closed the door behind him.

Caleb looked directly at me for the first time. "Joel told me he asked you out. I can't say the idea makes me happy, but it's probably the best thing, Molly," he said in a tired voice.

I could only nod my head.

"Did you reach the Raintrees?" he asked.

"No, I never got the chance. I didn't want to phone when

Joel was here. I suppose it's too late to be calling now, but we can do it first thing in the morning."

I was glad he would be there and glad I had waited. It wouldn't have seemed right to call without him.

"I never had a chance to tell you," I went on. "I had another encounter with Evaline last night. But not the girl Evaline. It was the older Evaline, the one you must have seen on the beach."

I decided not to mention how frightened I was when she held out her hand to me, or how she had approached me and touched my cheek. Caleb seemed too exhausted to deal with anything more. "She was on the porch. Then she just left," I finished. "It was before you came home."

He was standing above me on the first step, and I looked up to find him watching me. Under the overhead light, his eyes were hooded and cautious, deep green like the ocean at dusk.

"I'm sorry about last night, Caleb," I suddenly blurted before he had a chance to answer. "It wasn't fair to throw myself at you."

He looked at me a long time. Then he stepped down, even with me.

"You didn't throw yourself at me," he said slowly. "You offered me something I wish very much I could have accepted. You do know that, don't you?"

Again I could only nod. I didn't trust myself to speak.

"And I never got the chance to thank you for last night," he went on, his words coming slowly. "And the other times as well. But especially last night."

He lifted his hand to the back of my neck. "I've fallen in love with you, Molly," he said. "I never expected to, and I certainly never wanted to. But it happened in spite of everything . . . or maybe because of it. . . ." He bent his head and kissed me. His lips were warm, as was his hand on the back of my neck. Before I could react, he had turned and started upstairs.

Halfway up, he turned back to face me. "I want you to know, too, that if your mother wasn't coming home soon, tonight might be a very different story."

He started up again, limping slowly to the top. I could only stand at the bottom and watch him go. A sigh rose like a bird in my chest, beating there.

CHAPTER 17 ❧

MOTHER ALMOST CRAWLED off the ferry, as tired from her two days in New York as the rest of us were from our two days without her. The vaguest answers to her questions seemed to satisfy her. Until we got home.

Upstairs, she stopped me in the hall and cupped my chin in her hand, making me look directly into her eyes.

"Everything under control, Molly?" she asked.

I didn't even bother pretending I didn't know what she was talking about.

"Yes, Mother. Everything's under control." As much as I wished otherwise, it was the truth.

"For real?"

"Yes, Mother, for real," I answered with a sigh. She must have seen in my face that it was the truth because she kissed me and said good night.

"Saturday night I'm going out with Joel Bockman," I said just before she closed her door. "If that makes you feel any better."

"Actually, that does make me feel better."

"And, Mom, I'm glad you're home, too," I said.

With a little laugh, she closed her door behind her.

I went to bed wishing Caleb were there beside me and wondering if Evaline might come to my room again. If she did, I hoped it was the young girl and not the old woman. I wanted somehow to prove to her I could be her friend. But that night my sleep was uninterrupted.

The next morning we all slept late, and it wasn't until just before noon that I finally had a chance to call the Raintrees.

Both Mother and P.J. stayed around to find out what I learned. Caleb and I went into the hall to make the call, but when I picked up the receiver my stomach started churning.

"You do it." I held the phone out to Caleb. "I'm too nervous. If they don't know anything, I don't think I can stand it."

He shook his head. "If there is news, you deserve to hear it first. I think Evaline would want that."

I wiped my palms on my shorts, took a deep breath, and put through the call.

A man answered, identifying himself as Jerome Raintree. Before I'd finished explaining why I was calling, he interrupted.

"My housekeeper told me you'd be calling. Actually, it's my great-aunt Martha you'll want to talk to, Martha Bascombe. She's the great-granddaughter of Clara Raintree."

At the mention of the Raintrees' daughter, my heart skipped a beat. I wrote *Clara* on my pad of paper and underlined it. Beside it I wrote "Martha Bascombe — great-granddaughter." I showed the note to Caleb, who nodded and smiled, then turned my attention to what Jerome Raintree was saying.

"What little there is to know about Evaline Bloodsworth my great-aunt Martha knows better than anyone else. The family lost track of Evaline not long after she left, but because of the sad circumstances, her story was often mentioned.

"Sad circumstances?" I asked, and glanced at Caleb.

"Yes, but you'd better talk to Aunt Martha. There was also a letter, I believe."

"A letter?"

"Yes, I think Aunt Martha still has it. Before I give you her number, though, I'd like to ask why you're interested in Evaline Bloodsworth." He paused. "As far as I know, no one except our family knew about her."

As clearly as I could, I told him where we lived and that our house was on property where we thought Evaline had once lived. I mentioned the things we had found in the cabin and the diary.

"That's how I knew to call you," I explained. "She wrote about being sent to Lowell and living with Calvin and Minna Raintree. She mentioned they had two children, Clara and Thomas."

"Yes, I'm a direct descendant of Thomas. He was my great-great-grandfather. That's one advantage to having an old family that's always lived in the same town. The records are good. I didn't know there was a diary, though."

"It ends not long after Evaline came to Lowell," I went on. "So that's all we know. We wanted to learn more about her — how she happened to come back here."

"I told Aunt Martha about your call. She's willing to talk to you as long as you're not some nosy newshound just after a salacious story."

"Oh, no," I assured him, wondering what salacious meant. "I just became interested in Evaline because of her diary."

"I imagine Aunt Martha would like to see a copy of the diary. Maybe in exchange for a copy of the letter she has?"

"Oh, yes," I agreed quickly. "I'd be happy to do that."

He gave me her number, and I wrote it on my pad.

"Wait about thirty minutes before you call," he said. "I'll let her know you'll be calling and that it's all right to tell you what she knows of Evaline. She's eighty-five and a little hard of hearing, so the less you have to explain over the phone, the better."

"Thank you very much, Mr. Raintree. I really appreciate this."

"Happy I could be of help," he said. "She must have been a very lonely girl. It's nice to know someone's still interested in her."

"I — I want her to know she has a friend," I stammered.

"I'm sure she does," he said after a moment, in a gentle voice. "If you ever pass through Lowell, look us up."

"I certainly will, Mr. Raintree," I said with fervor, "and thanks again."

My hand was sweating as I set down the phone. I turned to Caleb. "He was nice, really nice, and his great-aunt Martha knows Evaline's story. I'm to call her in thirty minutes. He's going to let her know and tell her it's okay and she has a letter," I said all in one breath.

"It's going to take you that long to recover," Caleb said with a smile. He followed me into the kitchen, where I took a long drink of water and related everything Jerome Raintree had said to Mother and P.J.

"Imagine!" Mother said. "A letter still in existence. Is it a letter from Evaline herself?"

"I think that's what he said." I tried to remember his

exact words. "I think he said a letter to Clara Raintree. Or maybe it was to Minna."

In exactly thirty minutes, I went back to the phone and dialed the number he had given me. It was answered on the first ring, and I knew from the voice it had to be Great-aunt Martha Bascombe.

My conversation with her was more difficult because I had to repeat everything at least twice. Fortunately, Jerome Raintree had prepared her, and I didn't have to say too much. As she told me what she knew, I started to make some notes but soon stopped. It was not a story I would forget. By the time I hung up the phone, the sense of excitement and discovery had faded. I felt only a great sadness.

One look at me told Caleb something was wrong.

"What is it, Molly?" he asked, a look of concern on his face.

More than anything else, I wished I could tell him in private, but of course Mother and P.J. were waiting to hear. I poured myself a cup of coffee, and the four of us sat at the kitchen table exactly as we had the night I read the diary aloud. I began slowly, struggling to keep my voice even.

"Martha is Clara's great-granddaughter," I reminded them first and took a deep breath. "What she knows, she heard from her great-grandmother when she was a very young child. Clara gave her the letter to keep because she was the only girl in her family. She didn't say what happened to her mother or grandmother, and she doesn't know why Clara kept the letter so long or felt it was important. Maybe because Evaline was so pretty and paid special attention to Clara."

I took a sip of black coffee and swallowed, feeling it burn

all the way into my stomach. It tasted bitter. I concentrated on the dark liquid in the white cup. No one spoke or urged me on, and I was thankful.

"That was the first thing she said. Martha, I mean. She said her great-grandmother told her over and over how pretty Evaline was. With long, golden hair and blue eyes." It struck me that I had never seen Evaline in enough light to see the color of her eyes.

"Anyway," I went on, "Evaline had lived with the Raintrees and worked at the mill for just over a year when they found out she was pregnant."

I looked up and then quickly down again into my cup. "That man, her overseer, Mr. Dobbs, got her pregnant. Can you imagine a man taking advantage of a thirteen-year-old girl, knowing she was probably lonely and missing her family? He must have figured Evaline wouldn't dare fight him off, knowing he could fire her." My voice began to shake.

"Some things don't change, do they?" Mother said and reached over to touch my hand.

Unexpected tears welled up, and I blinked them away, bending over my cup to take another swallow of hot coffee.

"Of course she was fired anyway," I said when I could speak again. "As soon as the owner of the mill discovered she was pregnant, he fired her. Mrs. Raintree took pity on poor Evaline and let her stay. The Raintrees made Mr. Dobbs move out of the house, but he didn't even lose his job. Can you imagine — barely thirteen, pregnant, and all alone in the world?" Anger pushed away the tears that still threatened.

"The baby was born at the Raintrees' just before Evaline's fourteenth birthday. Mrs. Raintree found someone to take the baby, a couple she knew who didn't have children. They took the baby, and Mrs. Raintree kept Evaline until she was well enough to travel. She gave Evaline the fare home. She told her to tell her family she had gotten sick and couldn't work anymore and had to come home. And that's what Evaline did.

"They never heard anything more except for the one letter she wrote Clara shortly after she arrived home. That's the letter Martha Bascombe has. She didn't read it to me because she's sending me a copy. And I said I'd send a copy of the diary to her. We agreed."

"What an incredibly sad story!" Mother said after a moment. "That poor child!"

I couldn't look at Caleb.

I drained the rest of the coffee, afraid to put the cup down in the saucer because my hands were shaking. I tried to push away the memory creeping to the edge of my thoughts.

It was P.J. who opened the floodgates. "Jeez, what a crappy thing," he said. "She got fired and she didn't even get to keep her baby either."

Then the memory broke through — the dream of running down those endless corridors, searching for my baby and finding it too late. The dream of watching another woman claim the baby that should have been mine. I knew exactly how Evaline must have felt, the sense of loss and emptiness. The tears spilled over now, and nothing would stop them. I buried my head in my arms on the table, and I could only sit there and cry for Evaline and for myself and for the babies we both had lost.

Mother came around the table and put her arms around me.

"There, there, Molly," she crooned as she had when I was a child and came to her with some hurt. "Don't take it so hard. It was a long time ago."

She smoothed my hair with her hand.

I raised my head and looked up at Caleb, wishing Mother's arms were his arms. I could tell he, too, was remembering my dream, and in his face was all the love I had ever hoped to see.

CHAPTER 18 ⟨∾⟩

TWO DAYS LATER, on a gray, drizzly morning, the copy of the letter came. Both Mother and P.J. were in town when the mail was delivered, so I was able to read it in private. I read it three times, then went to the foot of the stairs to Caleb's attic room.

The door was ajar, and he was playing his guitar. I called up the stairs.

"Come on up, Molly."

He was on his bed, sheets of music composition paper spread around him. Beside him was the volume of poetry I had seen on the bedside table, open where the marker had been placed.

I held up the letter. "Look," I said. "The copy of Evaline's letter." I handed it to him.

He took one look and handed it back. "Read it out loud, Molly," he said with a smile. "You're better at figuring out her handwriting."

He cleared a space for me, and I sat at the end of the bed, remembering only too clearly the last time I had been there.

I unfolded the letter.

"It's dated February 3, 1827," I said and began to read:

Dear little Clara,

This is the letter I promised you. Perhaps you will share it with your mother. I want her to know how grateful I am for her kindness.

If it wasn't for your friendship and your mother's kindness, I don't know what I would have done. I remember the time we spent together so well. You were a sister to me while I was there and gave me much comfort. My life now is much as it used to be, but of course it can never be the same again, nor will I ever be the same.

I have regained much of my strength. I told my family I had been sick with influenza and needed to come home. I am grateful no one in New Dover knows the truth, and I pray they never learn it. I am filled with shame and sorrow.

I glanced at Caleb and cleared my throat. Then I went on.

The tears come less often now, and I am in hopes that one day this will all be behind me. But I will never have my baby back. I don't think I will ever marry although my mother tells me I must think of it since I will be fifteen my next birthday.

I pray my mother and father never learn the truth, for they would cast me out as a sinner.

I thank God, too, for your father's tolerance. Please let them know how grateful I am. I miss you, my little sister, and hope that one day we'll meet again. Pray for me.

I cleared my throat again. "Then she signs it, 'Your loving sister, Evaline.' There's a final postscript," I said. "A couple of lines written after her signature." I swallowed.

Because your mother knows the whereabouts of my baby, tell her I think of him often and long to know he is well. Perhaps her kind heart would allow her to inquire about him. It would set my heart at ease.

I folded the letter and carefully put it back in the envelope. "Poor Evaline," Caleb said softly. "Now we know what brought her back."

"But we still don't know what happened after that," I said. Now that the letter had come, I wanted to know the rest of the story more than ever. "We don't know how she happened to leave New Dover and come to Plum Cove Island — or when. And we don't know why she was shunned. I suppose it was because of the baby. But how did they find out?"

"Lowell's a long way away, and Evaline certainly wouldn't have told," Caleb said.

"And from what Mr. Bockman said," I went on, trying to fit more pieces into the puzzle, "it wasn't just that she didn't have friends. Everybody made such a point of avoiding her. Like she had the plague or something. Even back then, it must have been pretty common for unmarried girls to get pregnant."

"Those puritanical communities could be awfully vindictive."

"But they wouldn't have treated a girl like Evaline as if she were a leper, would they?"

The more I thought about it, the more indignant I became. What chance did a girl like Evaline have? If she felt totally alone, it was no wonder.

"I can't believe it was just the baby," I went on after a moment. "And anyway, how did they find out about it?"

Caleb smiled. "We seem to be right back where we started."

"And we still don't know what Evaline wants from us. Could it have to do with her baby?"

"Maybe," Caleb replied, "but somehow I don't think so. We couldn't do anything about that, anyway." He paused a moment, his forehead puckered in thought. "Maybe it's just the understanding she never got from the townspeople — or from her own family. A little forgiveness."

"Maybe so," I said slowly, thinking about it, and suddenly what Caleb suggested made sense. I remembered the sound of the crying I had heard outside in the night, the mournful cry of real despair. Forgiveness and understanding. Maybe that was exactly what Evaline was seeking. Or at least part of it. I remembered the old woman, the look of sorrow on her face, and the way she had touched me, and I shuddered. Although the young Evaline might have come to my room seeking forgiveness and understanding, I felt sure the old Evaline had come for quite another reason. But I had no idea what it was.

I looked at Caleb, thinking of what he had just said, remembering the injured rabbit and his nightmare. Clearly Caleb still hadn't forgiven himself, either.

A car turned into the drive. Mother wouldn't like finding me alone with Caleb in his bedroom in an empty house — even in the middle of the day. Reluctantly, I stood up and started toward the stairs.

That night, while Mother was busy in the kitchen and Caleb was working with P.J., on an impulse I went up to Mother's bedroom and put a call through to Chicago.

My father sounded especially pleased I had called, and without warning I found myself talking about Caleb. Once I started, I couldn't seem to stop. I told him about things we had done together, about Caleb's music and how talented he was, about the Judy Collins concert the coming week where he was going to play, about how much I liked being with him. About everything except what Caleb had told me the night of his nightmare — that, and how I really felt about him.

I stopped, suddenly aware I had revealed that, too.

"Still your Blabby, right, Daddy?" I said with a quavering little laugh.

"Still my little girl," he said. "But it sounds like you're growing up. It sounds like you . . . think a lot of Caleb."

"I guess I do," I said and took a breath. "Mother thinks I like him *too* much. Because we're double first cousins, I mean."

"That makes him almost like a brother, doesn't it?"

"I suppose it does."

"That could be a problem," he said. "That, and the fact that you're only seventeen, Molly. You've got all kinds of time ahead of you." He waited for me to respond, but the lump in my throat wouldn't let the words come. "That's not what you wanted to hear, though, is it?"

"I guess not," I said with another quavery laugh.

"I'd like to be able to tell you otherwise, Molly, you know I would. But I can't in all honesty do it. I can't tell you that what you do now won't make a difference later. Because it will. And I guess I just don't want to see you do something you may have serious regrets about sometime in the future."

His words sounded too familiar, and I remembered what Caleb had said that night in his room, about how sooner or later what we do comes back to haunt us and that we can't escape the choices we make.

"Have you ever done anything like that, Daddy?" I asked and felt tears spill over. "I mean something you couldn't forgive yourself for?" I stared out Mother's window and wiped my eyes with my sleeve, waiting for him to answer. It was a long time coming.

"Yes, sweetheart," he said at last. "I'm sorry to say, I have."

"What was it, Daddy?" I asked in a small voice and waited again.

"It was . . . it was giving up you and P.J.," he said. He cleared his throat. "That's something I'll never forgive myself for. Not the divorce, because there didn't seem to be any other solution. But a day doesn't go by that I don't regret not being with you and P.J." His voice caught and he coughed. "Especially tonight, Molly. I wish I could be with you right now."

"I wish you could, too, Daddy," I said with a sigh. "And I wish you could get to know Caleb again. I think you'd like him."

"I know I would," he said. "I always did. And remember one thing, Molly. . . ."

"What's that?"

"Remember that he can always be part of your life. He can always be close without being a . . . a lover." That word must have been hard for him to say.

"I know," I said. "I guess I just needed to hear someone else say it."

"Then I'm glad you called."

"Me, too," I said. "Good night, Daddy."

"Good night, honeybunch." He paused. "I guess it's true, then."

"What?"

"My little Blabby really has grown up." I heard him sigh before he set down the phone.

*

The first thing I noticed when I looked out my window the next morning was that the schooner had sailed out of the harbor. It seemed almost an omen of something coming to an end. The fact that it was Saturday didn't help my spirits, especially when Joel called at lunchtime to say he'd pick me up at seven-thirty.

After supper I went up to change. At exactly seven-thirty Joel pulled in the drive, and I met him at the door. Caleb was up in his room. The sounds of his guitar drifted through the open window.

Butch Cassidy and the Sundance Kid was playing at the Coronet, the only theater on the island. A few minutes into the movie, Joel reached over and took my hand. The skin of his palm was rough and callused like his grandfather's, but his hand was warm, not sweaty like a lot of the boys I had dated. His fingertips moved against my palm. I thought of how Caleb's fingers had traced the lines there.

At the end of the movie, Joel suggested we get something to eat before heading home. "The Whale's Belly's got the best hamburgers in town," he said, "if you don't mind going to a bar."

"I'll tell you a secret," I said with a laugh. "I've been wanting to go into the Whale's Belly ever since I was a kid and saw that sign posted in the window that says Booths for Ladies. I had great visions of the kind of place that would advertise *booths for ladies*. It sounded terribly raunchy."

"I'm afraid you're in for a big disappointment," Joel said with a wide grin.

We walked the half block down the street to the bar. The Booths for Ladies sign was still in the window, dirty and flyspecked after so many years of promise.

At ten on a Saturday night, the bar was crowded with a mixture of islanders and summer people who had started arriving by the ferry load since the Fourth of July. Before long the island, too, would be crowded.

We paused just inside the door, waiting for our eyes to adjust to the low level of light, and peered through the gloom to spot an empty table.

"Here you go," Joel said, taking my elbow and deftly steering me toward the last empty booth. "A booth for a lady." He slid into the seat across from me and watched me, smiling. "Is this what you always imagined it would be?"

"Hardly," I answered with a laugh. "I imagined something more like an opium den, I guess. You know, smoke-filled and full of dangling beaded curtains with sinister faces lurking behind them. And then somewhere, way in the back, two or three very proper booths where men weren't allowed to sit."

Joel threw back his head and laughed. "Wow! You had a vivid imagination for a — how old were you then?"

"Oh, maybe six or seven." I could feel myself blush.

"And already dreaming of hanging out in opium dens!

Well, you can see, the Whale's Belly is supposed to look more like the inside of a fish than an opium den. The typical nautical bar, I'm afraid. I hate being the one to spoil your dream."

"You haven't. I like this place fine."

The waitress came to take our order, a hamburger and Coke for me and a cheeseburger and beer for Joel.

When she had left, Joel leaned toward me, his face suddenly curious. "And what do you dream of now, Molly Todd? Now that you're all grown up."

That was the second time in two days I had been called "grown up." For some strange reason, it made me feel very young.

"Oh, lots of things," I said.

"Name one."

"Being an artist, I guess. A good one. After next year I want to go to art school. Maybe the Art Institute in Chicago. That way I could also see more of my father." Saying it out loud somehow made it seem more real. Like it really could happen.

"Caleb told me you're very talented. Better than his father."

I looked at him in surprise and tried to keep my voice light. "Oh, he was just being nice. Because I'm his cousin and all." It was the first time I'd ever heard Caleb question his father's talent, and I wondered if perhaps he was right and Uncle John simply wasn't good enough to succeed as an artist.

"There are a lot of artists around here," Joel went on, a hopeful look on his face. "This is a good place for artists to come. Even to live."

I thought again of Uncle John. It had seemed the perfect

place for him, but not perfect enough to support his family. I looked at Joel. He was watching me intently, as though he were expecting some kind of answer.

I groped for a way to change the subject.

"So how about you?" I asked. "What do you dream about?"

"I guess I don't have too many dreams," he said slowly. "Just what I'm doing. I like living here. I like being a fisherman. It's hard work in the summer, but it gives you lots of time in the winter. I have a woodworking business I've started. It's doing pretty good."

"What kind of woodworking?"

"Furniture mostly. I'm no Einstein, I guess, but I'm pretty good with my hands. Most of it's special orders for summer people that I work on over the winter."

"That's great, Joel," I said as the waitress set down our order. "It sounds like you've got your life all planned out. I envy you."

He picked up the catsup and looked at me over the top of the bottle. "Of course someday I'd like a family. You know, kids. And a wife, too," he added with a smile. "I guess the wife is supposed to come first, isn't she?"

I gave a little laugh. "These days it doesn't seem to make much difference," I said and took a bite of my hamburger. "Speaking of 'these days,'" I said casually, still searching for another topic, "has Caleb told you much about the war?"

"No. He doesn't talk about it. He talks a lot about being back. 'Home again,' he keeps saying, meaning the island. It's been good for him, I think, coming here. I wish he'd stay. Dad and I even offered him a place on the boat. We could use him. Dad would like to take it a little easier, and there's nobody I'd rather work with than Caleb."

"Did he say he would?"

"No, but he said he'd think about it."

My heart turned over at the possibility. Knowing Caleb would be here on the island every summer would be enough to get me through the winters.

"Oh, boy," he said suddenly and hit his forehead with his hand. "Grandpa gave me a message for you. He told me to be sure not to forget it, and I almost did."

Joel dug into his pocket and pulled out a piece of scrap paper.

"It's a woman's name," he said and handed it to me. "He said to tell you he thought she might know more about somebody called Evaline. He said you were interested in finding out what happened to her."

"That's right," I said cautiously. "We think she used to live on our property." I looked at the name scrawled on the slip of paper. Beside it was written *New Dover Nursing Home* and a telephone number.

"Letitia Hornsby?" I questioned, not sure I was reading the name right.

"Grandpa said he didn't even know she was still alive until someone mentioned her the other day. He said she's probably the only one left who might be able to tell you something. Her family lived the closest to your property. He said if anybody knew anything about this Evaline, it would be Letitia."

I carefully folded the paper and put it in my pocket, praying this woman held the key that would unlock the rest of Evaline's story. She would have to be very old.

Joel paid the check, and we started home. I was so engrossed in thoughts of Evaline that I was caught off-guard when Joel rounded the curve at High Point and pulled off the road by the old lighthouse. He parked in its shadow and turned to face me.

I braced myself, but he surprised me by not moving.

The darkness beneath the lighthouse was almost complete, but the whites of his eyes reflected what little light there was.

"I had a good time tonight, Molly," he began, his voice very soft. "You're very easy to be with."

He waited for me to make some kind of response.

I blurted the only thing that came to mind. "I had a good time, too, Joel." Dumb as it was, it seemed to satisfy him. He leaned back against his door, watching me.

"Sunday's the only day I don't have to go out with the boat," he said, "so Saturday night's my only free night. I'd like to do this again, though, as often as you're willing. That's assuming you *are* willing, of course." He smiled, his teeth gleaming white in the darkness.

I was just thankful he wasn't free seven nights a week. The sad part of it was, I liked him. He was fun to be with. If it hadn't been for Caleb, I probably would have been excited at the prospect of being Joel's girlfriend, and I wondered what might have happened if I had looked him up the summer before. I wondered if it would have made a difference.

"Sure, Joel," I said slowly, "but I'm afraid I can't next Saturday. The family's going over to New Dover." I emphasized family so he wouldn't expect me to invite him along.

"I know," he said, disappointment in his voice. "Caleb said you were all going to the Judy Collins concert. How about the next Saturday? There's a square dance in Bucks Harbor."

Square dancing sounded safe enough. "Sure," I said. "Sounds like fun."

"Great." He put his arm across the back of the seat, his hand on my shoulder. He pulled me to him and kissed me, a soft, lingering kiss. In the dark it was easy to imagine he was Caleb, and I closed my eyes and gave myself up to the kiss. Without thinking, I let my lips part. Joel's tongue reached out and touched mine, then moved over it, exploring. He gave a soft moan. My eyes blinked open and I drew back.

"We better go, Joel," I said quietly.

I prayed he wouldn't reach for me again, but it was myself I was angry with. I had led him on. The next time he would expect at least as much. I was a worse tease than Peggy Ann, and Joel deserved better. But what bothered me most was knowing that if he had been Caleb I wouldn't have pulled away at all.

"I'd better get home," I said again, staring out the front window at the black night.

"Sure," he said with a little sigh, and to my relief he shifted into gear. "Sometimes I forget you've got another year of high school, Molly. But you're right. There's no rush. We've got the rest of the summer and next summer, too, I hope."

"Yes, next summer, too."

I didn't want to think that far into the future. We drove the last half mile in silence.

"Thanks a lot, Joel," I said, slipping from the car as soon as he stopped in the drive. "Thanks for the nice evening. I'll see you in a couple of weeks."

" 'Night, Molly," he called as I swung the door closed behind me.

As I walked to the house, I glanced up at Caleb's room. His light was still on, his shadow outlined against the drawn shade as though he had been standing there listening for the sound of Joel's car bringing me home.

CHAPTER 19 ∽

THE NEXT DAY I wanted to take the ferry over to New Dover right away, but Mother talked me out of it.

"You can't just appear on the doorstep, Molly!" Her eyebrows shot up in exasperation. "It's a nursing home, not a hotel! You should call first. Make sure it's all right. Not to mention finding out if Mrs. Hornsby is willing to talk with you."

"She has to be willing," I said. "She just has to!"

I called the nursing home, only to be told Letitia Hornsby was recovering from bronchitis and it would be best not to come until the end of the week. Disappointed, I let my thoughts race ahead. "Let me check a minute," I said into the phone.

Holding my hand over the receiver, I called to Mother.

"They said the end of the week. Could we stop there before the concert?" I asked. "We'll be taking the car over, won't we?"

"Yes, I made a ferry reservation," Mother said, leaning against the kitchen door and wiping her wet hands on a dish towel. "That would work out just fine."

I took my hand off the receiver. "Could I come about five

o'clock next Saturday?" I asked and held my breath, waiting for the reply.

"That should be fine," the voice on the other end said. "But you'd better call first to make sure Mrs. Hornsby's well enough for visitors. Can I tell her who's coming?"

"My name is Molly Todd," I said. "I live on Plum Cove Island not far from where she used to live. She doesn't know me, but tell her I'd like to talk to her about Evaline Bloodsworth." A sudden horrible thought struck me. "Mrs. Hornsby isn't . . . I mean she . . . I mean, can she still remember things?"

A laugh came over the phone. "Letitia Hornsby? Remember? You bet your bottom dollar! Letitia doesn't get around like she used to. But her mind . . . well, I wish I was half as sharp!"

"Thank you!" I said with a heartfelt sigh of relief. "I'll call Saturday morning."

I hung up the phone, praying in every way I knew that she would recover quickly.

Caleb worked on his music all week. From time to time I could hear snatches of a haunting melody that made me pause to listen. Once I asked him what he was going to play Saturday night, but he just smiled and shook his head.

"Let it be a surprise," he said.

While he was busy, I filled the time by working on my drawing. I was on the final copy now, pleased at what was beginning to emerge.

At last Saturday came and I called the nursing home again, afraid I would hear that Letitia Hornsby was either dead or in a coma.

"Letitia's much better," the voice on the line said, and I

felt a rush of relief. "She's looking forward to talking with you."

"Great!" I almost yelled. "Thank you so much. I'll be there at five o'clock!"

A little after four-thirty, we drove off the ferry. The nursing home was just a mile from the center of town, set high in an open field with a view of the ocean below.

Caleb parked the Jeep in front and turned to face me in the backseat beside P.J. "Do you want us to go with you, Molly? Or would you rather go by yourself?"

"Perhaps you'd better go by yourself, Molly," Mother broke in. "She's not expecting anyone else. If she's been ill, she might not appreciate all of us descending on her."

Inside, I was relieved not to be asasaulted by the typical nursing-home odor of urine and strong disinfectant. The place looked freshly painted and well taken care of. At the front desk I was greeted by a woman of about forty with very bouffant blond hair.

"Oh, yes. You're here to see Letitia Hornsby," the woman responded with a smile when I identified myself. "Down the hall, to the left, then the third door on the right."

I walked down the hall, nervous, not knowing quite what to expect. At the first passageway, I turned left and found myself in a brightly lit hallway. Two elderly men were dozing in wheelchairs, heads bent, mouths open. One was snoring. I counted three doors and then turned and knocked softly. When there was no response, I knocked a little harder and was immediately rewarded with a clear "Come in."

Opening the door, I came face-to-face with Letitia Hornsby. She was sitting in a rocking chair in front of a window. The late-afternoon sun streamed in behind her, creating a soft white halo of hair around a thin, wrinkled face. I guessed her to be near ninety.

A blue crocheted shawl hung around frail shoulders, and an afghan covered her legs. "Come in, child," she said in a surprisingly strong voice and beckoned me with a hand covered with blue veins. "I've been expecting you."

I stepped into the room, and the door swung closed behind me. "I'm Molly Todd, Mrs. Hornsby," I said, nervously wiping my damp palms on my skirt.

"Yes, I know," she said and peered up at me. Under hooded, wrinkled lids, her blue eyes were sharp and piercing. She held out her hand, and I took it in mine, aware of how frail and thin the bones felt. I didn't want to squeeze them, and I stood there a moment, hand in hand with her, until she gestured to a chair nearby.

"I'm afraid that's the best I can offer you," she said with a smile.

I pulled it closer and sat down. "What a pleasant room this is," I said, looking around at the soft yellow walls that reflected the sun. They were hung with several prints of flowers, not particularly good artwork, but colorful. On the table beside her sat an array of photos, faded and brittle-looking.

"Yes, it's not a bad room — as such rooms go," she said with a little sigh. "So you've come from Plum Cove Island, is that right?"

"Yes, ma'am, from near Windhover."

"That's what they told me. Not far from my old home, I understand."

"I believe so. We have a house on the property where Evaline Bloodsworth used to live."

Her eyes narrowed and she looked past me. "Ah, yes.

Evaline Bloodsworth," she said slowly, and I held my breath, wondering if she remembered. "They said you were interested in Evaline." She looked back at me and shook her head slowly. "Poor, poor woman. Word was, her ghost had come back to haunt the place. But I never did hold much store in such tales."

"You never saw her, then? I mean her ghost, after she died?"

"No, I never did. I was the one who found her, though." She shook her head slowly from side to side.

"Found her?" I asked.

"Yes, when she died, poor woman. She was all alone, and my mother had sent me up the hill with some scraps of food for her. That was a bitter winter, I remember, colder than usual. My mother felt sorry for her, and we lived in the only house nearby." Letitia Hornsby's voice quavered. "I hadn't wanted to go that day because it was so cold and the wind was blowing something fierce. I was only eight at the time. But my mother sent me."

She reached out her hand and clasped mine, holding it lightly between her frail fingers. "Who told you I knew Evaline Bloodsworth?" she asked suddenly.

"Mr. Bockman," I said. "He said you were the only one who might remember her."

"Harry Bockman?" She gave a little laugh that rattled in her throat, a reminder of the bronchitis. "What a rapscallion he was as a boy! You tell him I remember that, too!"

"I don't think he's changed a whole lot, Mrs. Hornsby," I said and smiled. "But I'll be sure and tell him."

She glanced away, and her eyes dimmed as though the memories were beginning to fade.

"You were telling me about finding her," I prompted gently after a moment.

"Yes, that morning I went up and she was dead. Died with just a thin blanket wrapped around her. Whether she died of the cold or of natural causes, no one ever knew. She was an old woman by then. Almost as old as I am now," she added with a smile.

"Then you didn't know her very long?"

"Not long. Only the few years I carried food up to her. But she was always so kind. And such a lovely-looking woman, even that old. She had long, white hair. And skin as soft as a chamois. You could tell she must have been beautiful as a girl. Poor thing. I couldn't help but feel sorry for her, all alone. No one except us paid any attention to her."

"Do you know how she happened to come to Plum Cove Island?" I asked. "I mean, she lived here on the mainland. Do you know why she moved to the island?"

"Oh, yes indeed!" Mrs. Hornsby said, her voice rising and turning into a cough. When it subsided, she went on. "My mother made sure I knew why she came to the island! She told me Evaline was an example of how sinful ways could ruin a life. Poor Evaline was sent away from New Dover. Cast out."

"What had she done?" I asked, wondering if somehow word of her baby had followed her home.

"For one thing, it came to be known she had given birth to a baby, an illegitimate baby. When she was not even fourteen years old. That in itself was bad enough. But then she lied about it, tried to keep it a secret, and that's what the town couldn't forgive." Letitia Hornsby's fingers plucked at the afghan that had started to slip off her lap.

194

"Of course in those days no one ever admitted to things like that — or even talked about them. I suspect she was a reminder to a lot of folks of their own guilty secrets. But whatever the truth of the matter, in New Dover it was considered a curse even to talk to her, as though she contaminated the whole society."

A little frown deepened the wrinkles that ran down from Letitia's forehead. "So she was sent out of New Dover," she went on, "but when she came over to the island, no one there would have a thing to do with her either. People didn't even talk about her. It was as though she didn't exist. But my mother felt even a sinner should be allowed forgiveness and a little Christian charity. So I used to go up there from time to time, and I couldn't help but feel sorry for her."

I stared at Letitia, trying to imagine how it must feel to be so despised by your whole community.

"But Evaline couldn't have been the only girl in New Dover who had an illegitimate baby," I said. "What made her so horrible . . . so hated?"

At the urgency in my voice Letitia looked at me with sympathy.

"It's a sad story — almost too much to believe — not the kind of story I like to tell." She hesitated, glancing at me again quickly, but continued. "When Evaline first came home from Lowell, she kept to herself. As pretty as she was, she paid no mind to any of the local boys. After a while they stopped paying her court. By age thirty, she was a confirmed spinster, still living at home with her parents."

She cleared her throat and picked at a loose thread in the shawl.

"A year or so later, a new road was planned that would run right past New Dover. The men to work the road came to town, but there wasn't a hotel in town then, so they had to be put up at local houses. The young man in charge of laying out the road stayed with the Bloodsworths. As my mother told it, he was a handsome young man, not yet twenty, and for all the difference in their ages, he and Evaline fell madly in love. Not long after, they married."

She stopped again, her eyes shifting nervously around the room. I could tell she was uncomfortable telling me the story and waited quietly for her to continue. At last she took a deep breath and went on.

"Well, after the marriage the young man invited his family to come to New Dover and meet his new bride. But when they came and were introduced to Evaline and heard her full name, they knew the worst had happened." She coughed again and looked at me with her sharp eyes. "As it turned out . . . well, it seems Evaline was not only the young man's wife but also his mother."

I stared at Letitia, unable to say a word. The horror of what she was telling crept through me, numbed my brain.

"Less than twenty years earlier," she went on after a moment, "this family had adopted a baby boy. They knew nothing about him except the name of the mother. They never told their son he was adopted or who his mother was. And because they kept silent, this was the very woman the young man fell in love with and married."

I continued to stare at her, still trying to comprehend what she was telling me.

"What happened to him?" I whispered after a long silence.

"As soon as they found out, his family took him back to Massachusetts. The marriage was annulled. As best is known, that was the last Evaline ever saw or heard of him.

It was like he dropped off the face of the earth. It must have broken Evaline's heart. She lost her son not once but twice. And when the people of New Dover found out — about the baby and the lies and the marriage — that was when she was sent away and came to live by herself on Plum Cove Island."

"But why did they blame her so much?" I whispered, still not trusting my voice. "Evaline couldn't have *known* she was his mother!"

"Knowing or not knowing didn't finally matter. It just wasn't right. Lord, child, these people were farmers mostly. They didn't even mix up their animals that way. For breeding, they took their males and females from different sources. Inbreeding always produced bad stock — it just wasn't considered right. So for a mother and son to marry — even not knowing — was more than the town could tolerate."

I tried to push her words aside, but they bored into me.

Letitia went on, her voice very gentle now. "Evaline was distraught at the young man's leaving and grieved for him openly. So as well as her failure to confess to the earlier sins, it was the incestuous marriage and her failure to repent it that the town couldn't forgive."

She paused for a moment, shaking her head slowly back and forth, as if reflecting on the tragedy of Evaline's life. "But even knowing all the wrong she had done, the morning I found her, I couldn't help but weep for her. So sad she always was, and so alone."

Her eyes misted at the memory. Seeing her eyes wet with tears made my own eyes fill.

"Goodness, child," Letitia said after a moment and reached for two tissues. She handed one to me. "Aren't we a pair? Crying over something that happened so long ago."

"Thank you," I whispered. "Thank you so much for telling me."

She patted my hand. "My dear girl," she said, "I'm happy you cared enough to come. Company is always welcome. A person gets lonely here. I hope you'll come again. Whenever you can."

"I'd like that," I said.

"It makes me feel better knowing poor Evaline hasn't been shunned altogether."

"No," I said. "She isn't shunned. Not anymore. I promised her that." I rose from the chair.

Letitia looked up at me, her bright eyes questioning.

"So you've seen her, have you?" she asked in a quiet voice. I nodded.

Her eyes held mine, and she looked right into me.

"And you carry a secret, too," she said.

I nodded again. In a daze I walked to the door and opened it. I turned back to find her still watching me.

"If you ever see Evaline again," she said, "tell her I remember her. Tell her she's forgiven."

"I'll tell her," I said softly, and closed the door behind me.

CHAPTER 20 ∾

"OH, YUCK!" P.J. said and stuck out his tongue, a look of distaste scrunching up his face, pushing his glasses up on his nose. "That's gross!"

We had driven from the nursing home to the New Dover Music Theater and spread a blanket on the grass below the stage to eat our picnic supper before the concert. Reluctantly, I had told them the rest of Evaline's story. That was P.J.'s response — yuck. I was sorry I hadn't come the day before to see Letitia Hornsby by myself.

Last winter our class had read *Oedipus Rex,* another of Mr. Daniels's favorites. Some of the class had reacted pretty much the same way. Yuck. Gross. What guy could be that hard up? What geek would want to sleep with his own mother? — until Mr. Daniels shot them an icy glare and told them to remember they were in English class, not the locker room, and if they didn't have anything intelligent to say, shut up.

At first I hadn't felt too much different, but then I began to sympathize with Oedipus. After all, the Fates had decreed it, and he hadn't known Jocasta was his mother. Besides, it was a myth, a story to teach a lesson about human nature and pride and guilt and sins-of-the-fathers and all those other ideas Greek tragedies are always about. It wasn't something that could *literally* happen.

Now I was discovering it could.

"It's not 'yuck,' P.J.," I said, rising to Evaline's defense. "After all, Evaline's son wasn't even fourteen years younger. They didn't know they were mother and son. Any more than Oedipus and his mother."

"Who were they?"

"Oedipus was a Greek king who killed his father and married his mother."

"Gross!" P.J. looked sideways at Mother, who only smiled. "Besides, how could they not know?"

"Maybe that's exactly why they fell in love," I protested. "Maybe their blood ties were so close they had a special feeling about each other without knowing why. Maybe that's what made the relationship so special and why they fell in love — "

I stopped abruptly, aware of the hole I was digging for myself. I felt Mother's eyes fixed on me, boring into me. I glanced at Caleb, but he wouldn't meet my gaze.

I thought of the two Evalines, the young girl who had given birth to a secret illegitimate child and the woman who had later married that child. I thought, too, of Letitia's words and was sure now that Caleb had been right — that the young Evaline was searching for forgiveness so that at last her spirit could rest.

But my thoughts continued back to the night of the Fourth of July, the night the old woman had appeared. I remembered the look in her eyes, the touch of her finger, and I suddenly knew she had come to warn me about the loneliness and grief she had experienced, to warn me about my feelings for Caleb. But like Mother, Evaline's warning had come too late.

P.J. was staring at me, openmouthed at my outburst. Of course he would feel as he did. If I were a ten-year-old boy, I'd have felt the same way. At that age everything is black or white.

I was spared having to say anything further by the crackle of the loudspeaker and the announcement that all those interested in performing before the concert began should come backstage for instructions.

Caleb rose stiffly, picked up his guitar, and climbed the steps to the stage.

He didn't appear the least bit nervous, but I was. I looked around at the crowd that had gathered, and my stomach turned over. Since we had arrived the entire hillside had filled with people. Some were stretched out on blankets, some had brought folding chairs, and some just sat on the grass, but every available space was taken. I was glad we had gotten there early enough to get a spot near the stage.

The sun had dropped behind the hill, spreading a dark shadow across the eastern slope. A half-moon gleamed, at first palely, then more deeply as the sky grew darker. The stage lights dimmed up. I was beginning to worry that Caleb wasn't coming back when he suddenly appeared from the side and sat down again beside us.

"They're letting us each do two songs because there's only four of us," he said with a smile. "We're the warm-up for Judy Collins, and we're supposed to fill forty-five minutes. We start at eight. She comes on at eight-forty-five."

"When do you go on?" P.J. asked.

"I go last," Caleb said. "We drew numbers. Luckily I got

four. They're going to call us up from the audience one at a time."

"Why aren't you a basket case?" I blurted out. "How can you be so calm?"

"I don't know," he said, as though thinking about it for the first time. "I guess because it's something I enjoy doing so much. You just lose track of what's going on around you." He looked at me and smiled. "You must feel that way when you're really into a drawing."

"Sure, but I don't have an audience to worry about!"

He shrugged. "For me, the audience makes it that much better. I can't really explain why."

P.J. looked at him with awe, and I knew I was a mirror image of P.J. at that moment. This was such a different Caleb from the one I had seen the night of his dream. I didn't know which one touched me more.

"I could never play in front of people," P.J. said in a small voice.

"Sure you could." Caleb reached over and rested his hand lightly on the top of P.J.'s head. P.J. smiled, and a jealous twinge went through me as I watched them. Somehow P.J. always brought out the softer side of Caleb.

A man walked out to center stage and stood in front of the microphone. A spotlight flickered and found him. Gradually the crowd began to quiet.

"Welcome to the New Dover Outdoor Music Theater," the man began. The crowd applauded, cheered, and stomped their feet.

"Tonight we have a double treat for you. Judy Collins —" more stomping and cheering, " — and four talented young performers who are here to entertain you now. Let's give them a warm welcome."

The applause swelled, then died again as the MC announced the first of the group, a girl in her midtwenties. She got off to a shaky start, but the audience was polite and gradually, as she gained confidence, she settled into her music. She played an electric guitar and sang two numbers from *Hair*.

The next two were men, one really no more than a boy, younger than I. He wasn't bad, but the other one played classical guitar, and it sounded like the same thing over and over.

By the time Caleb was announced, the crowd was growing restless. He climbed the steps and walked to the microphone, his limp barely noticeable. I closed my eyes and said a little prayer. "Please, please, please," I whispered, but whether it was to God or Caleb or the audience, I couldn't be sure. All of the above, I decided.

"I'd like to dedicate these two songs to my father," Caleb said quietly into the mike, but his voice carried clearly across the stretch of grass and up the hill. Settling himself on the stool, he glanced down at Mother and began the first song without announcing it. Mother's face was very still.

I took a deep breath and held it, afraid by now the audience wouldn't quiet down for anyone but Judy Collins.

He played three chords, then sang the opening line of James Taylor's "Fire and Rain." Everyone knew the song and probably knew, too, that he had written it for a friend who had died.

Caleb's voice rang out across the dark hillside, the clear tenor that sent chills up my spine every time I heard it.

Before he had finished the first line, the murmurs of the crowd were dying down. Faces turned to watch him, a thousand pale moons gleaming in the reflected light of the stage.

My breath escaped with a slow sigh. I turned as well, riveted now on that solitary figure on the stage.

By the time he began the first chorus, a little current rippled through the crowd. They knew they were hearing something special. And by the time he came to the last plaintive line about always thinking he'd see his friend again, there wasn't a sound. Then the applause began, rolling down the hill to the stage like a wave nearing the shore. I began to relax.

When the applause faded, Caleb announced his second song and took me by surprise.

"This is also for my father," he said, and by now everyone was listening. "It's a song I wrote to a poem by the Irish poet William Butler Yeats. I call it simply "Innisfree.""

He played the opening notes, and the crowd grew still. The melody was the one I'd heard in snatches through his window, haunting, the kind that runs through your head long after it has stopped. It wasn't in a minor key, but it made me think of the feeling of melancholy, lovely and harmonious, that sometimes overtakes you as you watch the sun slip below the horizon after a perfect day. The audience felt it, too, and listened as he sang the words of the Yeats poem.

I will arise and go now, and go to Innisfree,
And a small cabin build there of clay and wattles made.
Nine bean-rows will I have there, a hive for the honeybee,
        And live alone in the bee-loud glade.

And I shall have some peace there, for peace comes
            dropping slow,
Dropping from the veils of the morning to where the
            cricket sings;

*There midnight's all a glimmer, and noon a purple glow,
    And evening full of the linnet's wings.*

*I will arise and go now, for always night and day
I hear lake water lapping with low sounds by the shore;
While I stand on the roadway, or on the pavements grey,
    I hear it in the deep heart's core.*

He repeated the last line three times, each time slower and softer than the last. When he came to the end, it wasn't much more than a whisper, but in the silence, every syllable was audible.

The applause rose around us. I could only sit there, not even able to clap. All my feelings surged up, rising to my face, so that when at last Caleb looked down at me and our eyes met, he could read them all there. The corners of his mouth turned up, green sparks lit his eyes. The lines in his face relaxed, and in the brightness of the spotlight I saw my own longing reflected in the softness of his expression.

His eyes closed. When they opened again, he looked out at the audience and rose from the stool to acknowledge their applause.

The MC moved into the wing and gestured to Caleb until he caught his attention. He mouthed a message. Caleb raised his eyebrows in question then nodded. The man backed off a few steps and disappeared into the shadows of the wing. A woman stepped forward and took his place, a woman with long, brown hair, not as dark as mine but straight like mine. Judy Collins had come into the wings to listen before her entrance.

Caleb sat back down on the stool, and the crowd quieted.

"Because this evening is for my father," he said in his quiet voice, "I'd like to sing this last song for him as well.

It was his favorite." He looked at Mother, sitting directly below him. "Aunt Libby?"

Mother stared up at him, her face expressionless. Then she nodded, her chin moving very slowly down and up again.

This time I wasn't surprised. He played the opening bars of "The Londonderry Air" and began to sing the lyric "Danny Boy." As I listened to Caleb sing it in his strong, true tenor, I thought of Uncle John and looked at Mother.

She was sitting with her knees drawn up. Her elbows rested on her knees, so that her hands formed a cradle for her face and hid it. I thought she must be crying and didn't want P.J. or me to see her, but at the end of the song, when the crowd broke into applause once more, she lifted her face and her eyes were only misted. She looked suddenly young again.

Caleb walked down from the stage, and the applause continued. As he made his way through the people to our blanket, Mother stood up. She moved to him and as they met, her arms went around him and they stood in a silent embrace. Mother was the first to move. She let her arms slowly fall and took a step back.

"Thank you, Caleb," she said in a voice I barely heard. "I never would let myself admit . . . to what he had done. I never would allow myself to grieve because it would have been admitting . . . but I loved him very much. Now I think I can begin to grieve. I can begin to let it go."

P.J. suddenly lunged forward and threw his arms around Caleb's legs, almost toppling him.

"You were stupendous!" he said in a loud voice that made the people around us laugh.

It seemed that I was the only one who couldn't get up and throw my arms around him.

He came and sat beside me. I reached out two fingers and touched his wrist, pressing them lightly against his flesh, feeling the bone and the quickness of his pulse beneath my fingertips. His heartbeat matched mine.

Neither of us moved, not even when the MC came out to announce Judy Collins. Not even when the audience stomped and hooted, applauding wildly as she came onstage and stood in the spotlight.

She was dressed in a long, embroidered skirt and high-necked blouse. Her brown hair hung straight down her back and gleamed in the light. Her face, without makeup, looked pale under the bright spotlight, but when she smiled it glowed. The applause died down when she began to speak into the microphone.

"Now I know why they call it a 'warm-up,' " she said, lightly strumming the strings of her guitar. "You can't get much warmer than that, can you? He's a hard act to follow!" She laughed and the audience applauded. Caleb looked up at her and smiled.

"Without further ado," she went on, "I'd like to sing for you. Some of your old favorites and some new ones, too."

For the next hour she sang without pause. Some of the songs I knew well, some were familiar, others I hadn't heard before.

She sang a song called "Albatross" I didn't know. I thought of the mariner and the schooner in the harbor that had set sail the week before.

For her final number she sang "Suzanne," my favorite of all her recordings. I especially liked the second verse and listened closely as she sang it.

And Jesus was a sailor when he walked upon the water
And he spent a long time watching
From a lonely wooden tower
And when he knew for certain
That only drowning men could see him,
He said, "All men shall be sailors, then,
Until the sea shall free them. . . ."

I had never been certain exactly what those lines meant, but as I listened to them this time, I began to sense that somehow they were about Jesus, who, because he had suffered, could understand the suffering of the hopeless and the lost, the "drowning men." He could forgive them, no matter what their sins.

It made me think of Uncle John and Evaline, and Caleb, too, and I pressed my fingers into the flesh of his wrist.

Only at the very end did Caleb and I raise our hands from the blanket to applaud. The audience wouldn't let her go. They wanted more. Finally she came onstage again and stepped to the microphone once more. A hush fell.

"You've been such a nice audience," she said, "I'd like to do one final number for you. It's a song I recently recorded, and I know it will be familiar to many of you."

Very softly, with no guitar accompaniment, she began to sing "Amazing Grace." Our junior-senior a cappella choir had sung it for graduation, and I knew it well.

Amazing grace, how sweet the sound . . .

As she sang the first verse and moved into the second, the audience began to sway in time to the music, as though joined together by an invisible thread.

She started the third verse. Like a bird, her voice rose in

the still night, touching all of us like a blessing. When she came to the final verse, she asked the audience to sing with her and lined the lyric for them.

> *When we've been there ten thousand years,*
> *Bright shining as the sun,*
> *We've no less days to sing God's praise*
> *Then when we'd first begun.*

The voices rose in unison. Those who didn't sing, hummed the melody. The sound overflowed the theater and spilled into New Dover, floating out across the ocean and over the whole world, it seemed.

Then she reprised the first verse, everyone joining in, and one by one the people in the audience rose and joined hands, each person clasping the hands of the people who stood on either side. I held Caleb's and P.J.'s, and on the other side of P.J., I saw an elderly woman reach over and take his free hand. And Mother, too. On one side, she clasped Caleb's hand, on the other, the hand of a stranger. We stood there, a human chain of hands touching, swaying together, humming the melody as Judy Collins's voice rose in the harmony.

The song came to an end, but for a long time no one moved.

At last Judy rose from the stool. "Thank you all," she said softly into the microphone. "God bless you, and good night."

The lights dimmed, and she walked offstage into darkness. The crowd stood in silence. No one wanted to let go of the hands they still held. I least of all.

209

CHAPTER 21 ∽

THE CROWD SLOWLY began to drift up the hill toward the parking area. We gathered our things and folded the blanket, waiting for the jam to thin out before trying to make our way to the car.

A man came to the edge of the stage, leaned over the apron, and beckoned to Caleb. As Caleb approached him, the man said something I couldn't hear. A look of surprise crossed Caleb's face. He nodded and turned.

"I'll be right back," he said. "You three go ahead. I'll meet you at the car."

"Don't be long, Caleb," Mother called after him. "We can't miss that last ferry."

Caleb nodded and disappeared into the darkness around the side of the proscenium.

"What a great concert!" P.J. said as we started up the hill. "They oughta pay Caleb. He was just as good as Judy Collins."

"Just about," Mother said.

Better, I thought.

"What do you suppose they wanted him for?" I asked, wondering why it was that every time he left, I worried I wasn't going to see him again.

"The manager probably wanted to thank him," Mother said.

By the time we reached the car and loaded it, the crowd had thinned and the parking area was less congested. We spotted Caleb as he reached the top of the hill, and Mother drove to the end of the field and picked him up.

"Thanks for waiting, Aunt Libby," he said as he climbed into the front seat beside her.

"Did they pay you, Caleb?" P.J. asked, hanging over the seat.

"Even better," Caleb said, smiling. "Judy Collins's manager was there. He gave me his card. He said if I was ever in New York to look him up. That maybe we could work together."

"Oh, Caleb, that's phenomenal!" I burst out, leaning over the seat myself. "He wants to sign you?"

"It's a possibility."

"Far out!" P.J. shouted, and his glasses flew off the end of his nose. "A celebrity!"

"Not quite, P.J. Don't get carried away. He didn't make any promises. Just said come to see him." Caleb turned to look at P.J. and caught my eye. Even in the dim glow from the dashboard, his eyes were full of light.

"He'll sign you," I said.

"I think it sounds exciting," Mother said. "No matter what comes of it, Caleb, it's a beginning. A goal to move toward."

Something in the tone of her voice and the look she and Caleb exchanged filled me with sudden apprehension. I didn't want to think about what might come after signing with an agent or even what it might mean. I only wanted to think about how happy Caleb seemed at that moment.

By the time we'd driven onto the ferry and parked the Jeep on the car deck, P.J. was almost asleep. I climbed out, and he stretched out along the backseat. Mother had bought a newspaper on the dock and went to sit in the cabin to read it. Caleb and I stayed outside. I walked to the stern and leaned against the rail. Caleb came and stood beside me. Neither of us spoke as we looked down into the black, oily water beneath us.

"Wait here a minute, Molly," he said after a moment. "I'll be right back."

He went into the cabin and sat down beside Mother. She looked at him and folded her paper. Seeing their faces at a distance, side by side, I was aware for the first time of the resemblance between them and of how much Mother looked like Uncle John. If looks were what counted, Mother could have been Caleb's mother, just as Aunt Phoebe could have been my mother. I found the thought disturbing and turned back to the rail.

For the first time since the concert had begun, I thought of Evaline and the sadness of her life. It seemed so unfair for one person to bear such a heavy burden and so unfair that life or fate or whatever it is that seems to direct our destinies dealt her such a rotten hand. Poor Evaline had been a pawn of forces beyond her control — a whim of nature and an especially hard year, the poverty of her family, the desire of a stranger, and finally, the cruelty of having the only man she ever loved be the son she had borne. Somehow, I wanted to make it up to her.

The engine started. Beneath me the water churned into a pale, creamy froth as the ferry slowly pulled away from the dock. I was deep in thoughts of Evaline when the cabin door closed and Caleb came back to the rail to stand beside me.

He leaned closer. His shoulder pressed against mine. For a moment we stood in silence, shoulders touching, our hands dangling over the rail. We stood together, so close there was no division between us. I leaned into him, wanting to feel more intensely the weight of his body against mine.

"There's something I have to tell you, Molly," Caleb said in a low voice. "Something I didn't mention earlier."

I turned my head to look at him, but he was still staring at the water. I waited.

"A friend of Judy Collins was there tonight. A disc jockey from Boston. He offered me a spot on his show. A chance to come and be interviewed and sing live on FM."

"Caleb, that's wonderful!" I cried. "When?"

"Next Saturday. On his late-afternoon show. It means I'd have to take the early-morning ferry and fly out of Bangor to Boston."

"You're going to do it, aren't you?" I said. "You'd be crazy not to. It's a great chance. And you could fly back again Saturday night." I stopped, puzzled by his hesitancy. "You *are* going to go, aren't you?"

"Yes, I'll go," he finally said. "You're right, I'd be crazy not to. But I'm not going to come back, Molly."

"Not come back?" I repeated. My insides slowly began to crumple, folding over and over like a piece of discarded newspaper.

"It only makes sense that I go down to New York right away and see if the manager's offer means anything. I'll fly directly to New York from Boston."

"But you could come back after that."

"I don't think so, Molly."

"But you were going to spend the summer with us! And you've only been here three weeks!"

He looked at me for the first time. "I know. And look what happened in those three weeks."

"You could come back, Caleb, after you see about it!"

"No, Molly, I can't. Not for a while."

"Why? Why can't you?" I cried, not wanting to hear what I knew he would say.

He turned back to the water as though searching for the words in the black swells of the waves.

"The night you came to my room, Molly," he began slowly, "I came very close to — well, we both know what almost happened. After you left, I promised myself it would never happen. And now I'm afraid if I stay any longer I'll break that promise."

"But would that be so terrible?" I whispered, my voice breaking.

"Yes, I think it might. I've got enough to answer for, Molly, without adding you to my list of victims."

"I'm hardly your 'victim'! And neither was Robert Englehart or those Vietnamese. You did what you had to do. Sometimes the choices are just lousy ones!"

"Oh, Molly," he said with a little laugh, "I hate to think what would have become of me if you hadn't been here this summer."

"Then don't leave, Caleb! Don't stay away!"

"I have to. At least for a while. Your mother thinks it's best, too."

"You told Mother?" For a moment my outrage almost filled the huge emptiness inside of me. "You told her — all of this?"

"She knows, Molly," he said gently. "She's known all along. She can see what's been happening. I guess I just wanted her to know that . . . that nothing had happened while she was gone. But she can see what will happen if I stay, and she's right. If I were in her place, I'd send me packing. She's too kind for that, so the best thing I can do is leave of my own accord."

"But would it really be so terrible?" I whispered again. "I mean, if you were to stay . . . if we were to . . ."

"It could be, Molly. For both of us. But especially for you. Evaline's story should be enough to make us aware of that. But it isn't just that we're cousins."

"What, then?"

His eyes closed, and his voice dropped so low I had to strain to hear him. "Molly, you don't know how much I want to stay . . . how much I want to love you. I've never felt like this, and I don't know exactly what to do about it. But I know my life's been pretty messed up, and for the first time in a long time, things are beginning to make sense again. I have a lot still to take care of, though, and it's going to take some time. I'm twenty-one, Molly, but you're only seventeen."

There was that phrase I dreaded. I looked away.

"You've got your whole life ahead of you, Molly, and it'd be wrong to take any of those years or those experiences away from you. Eventually you'd resent it. And that's the last thing I want."

I thought of my father. Caleb's words sounded too familiar.

"You've got another year of high school, and then coll — art school." I looked at him, and he smiled. "You know yourself you don't want to give that up. You shouldn't. It's too important. It's what you are, Molly. It's part of what makes you so special."

"Like your music," I said after a moment.

"Yes. Like my music. And I haven't had a chance yet to try that out. To see if it will work. We both need time, Molly."

I suddenly remembered Joel's offer.

"Joel said they offered you a place on the boat, a chance to take over for Mr. Bockman. Would you ever come back and do that?"

"Maybe. Someday. I still feel this is my home."

If the island were still his home, and if I came here every summer. . . . For the first time since we had started talking, I felt a glimmer of hope.

"Who knows?" Caleb went on. "Maybe someday I'll do both. Be a musician and a fisherman, too."

I felt another rush of hope. "Joel says he's a fisherman in summer and a furniture maker in winter. So it's possible."

"That's another thing," he said slowly. "We both need to take some time to . . . be with other people. You, especially. Joel thinks a lot of you. Will you see him after I leave?"

I thought of the following Saturday night and winced. "It will be hard not to, I suppose," I said.

"Well, you should. And when you go away to school, too."

"It won't make a difference in how I feel."

"But you don't know that, Molly. And you need to know. Then, maybe someday, when we have some time and distance behind us, we'll discover we can be very good friends." His fingers reached and touched mine. "And there's nobody in this world I would rather have as a friend."

I hung onto his words, tucked them away in a safe place in my heart where every now and then, when I missed him most, I could pull them out again and hear him say "maybe someday."

It all came down to making choices, I thought. But the important thing was being able to make those choices. Not like Uncle John, who felt he had no choice left. Or Evaline, whose choices ended at age twelve when she was sent away only to be seduced.

Or perhaps she had wished for that, even as I had wished for it that night in Caleb's room, wished for it now.

"Do you suppose it's possible Evaline wanted that man to make love to her?" I asked and looked at Caleb. "That maybe she was so unhappy and lonely she longed for . . . for any human touch?"

"If that's true," Caleb said softly, "it makes it all the sadder."

"Yes," I said. "And I made Evaline a promise, too, Caleb. Before you go, we have to do something for her. I told her we wouldn't forget her."

"What is it you want to do?"

"I don't know exactly. But what you said earlier, about understanding and forgiveness, maybe that's what we should try to give her somehow."

Caleb looked at me. "You mean, like an exorcism?"

"Yes, but not exactly," I said, trying to sort out in my mind just what I did mean. "Exorcism gets rid of an evil spirit. Evaline's spirit certainly isn't evil, no matter what the people of New Dover thought. We need to put it to rest somehow."

Caleb shook his head. "I don't know of a service for that. And I'd feel funny fooling around with an actual church service, anyway. I think it would have to be something we did just for her that's not tied to any church." He smiled. "I've got enough to answer for without being guilty of blasphemy, too."

"It's important, though, that we do this together, Caleb — before you leave." I couldn't bring myself to think about that. "That very first day, when we saw her down near the beach, it was you she was looking at. I think it's important for you to be there."

I suddenly wondered if Evaline had appeared because she felt Caleb was a kindred spirit, someone who shared the same heavy burden of guilt she had carried so long.

"All right," Caleb said, "we'll work on it this week. Whatever we come up with, we'll do it Friday."

Now that Caleb had agreed, the thought of what we were attempting made me suddenly nervous. We were dealing with things way beyond our knowledge or experience, and I wasn't sure we might not regret it. But when I thought of Evaline, who had been without a friend so much of her life, I knew I couldn't fail her this time. At least not without trying.

I had a sudden idea. "We should do this out in her cabin," I said.

He nodded.

"And just the two of us? Please?"

"Just the two of us," he promised.

The shore lights of Bucks Harbor were growing brighter.

Above, the light of the half-moon softened the water where our shadows rippled. The stream of light from the cabin behind us cast deeper shadows on the water, dividing our bodies into light and darkness but not one from the other.

Ahead, the lights of the island's ferry dock glimmered in the darkness, welcoming us home.

CHAPTER 22 ∽

URING THE NEXT WEEK, what I felt wasn't so much
pain as a hollowness, like a drum with the skin stretched
tight. Sunday morning, when P.J. learned Caleb was leaving,
he broke down in tears and for the rest of the day attached
himself to Caleb like the shadow he had been during the
first days after Caleb's arrival. Caleb made a point of check-
ing with the music store in Windhover and found someone
who taught guitar. He persuaded Mother to let P.J. continue
with lessons. As the days passed, P.J. gradually came to
accept the fact of Caleb's departure. He at least had Roger.

On Tuesday and Thursday, Caleb went out in the boat
with Joel. As much as I wanted him at home, I couldn't
begrudge Joel the chance to persuade Caleb to become his
partner. I prayed he would succeed, if not for the rest of
this summer, at least for the summers to come.

While Caleb was fishing, I worked on the drawing. The
first day, I went out to the cabin but found it hard to con-
centrate. I caught myself looking up from my work, listening
for Evaline, anticipating that rush of air that indicated her
presence. I never felt it, but I sensed she was there.

I made so little progress that on Thursday I decided to
stay home and work out on the veranda. In the early after-

noon I completed the drawing with a few final, careful strokes across the shadowed side of Caleb's face, a light hatching of fine lines with the pen. Then I began on the color. Just a dab of watercolor here and there. A touch of green in Caleb's eyes and on the shutters of the house. A wash of blue behind the schooner and over the cluster of pines. A streak of red-brown across the guitar Caleb was holding. That was all.

Mother came out as I was adding the last touch of color. She stood behind me and looked at the drawing over my shoulder, not speaking. I took a step back and, side by side, we looked at it together. It was exactly the way I had envisioned it.

She put her arm around my shoulders. "Oh, Molly," she said at last, "so much love. How could I have let this happen?"

Neither of us moved. I swallowed hard, but it was a long time before I could answer.

"If it hadn't happened — that's the only thing that would have made me sorry," I said.

"I know how much it must hurt right now."

"Of course it does. But that doesn't make me sorry it happened." I looked at her. "You loved Uncle John. The fact that he died doesn't make you sorry he was ever your brother."

"Of course not," she said, and her eyes were filled with sadness. "The years we grew up together, I wouldn't have given up those years for anything . . . not even knowing how they ended."

"That's exactly how I feel," I whispered.

It was the first time we had ever spoken of Uncle John's

death. Mother lifted her hand and touched my cheek. From between us, a great weight seemed to lift.

*

On Thursday night Joel came home with Caleb and had supper with us, his good-bye to Caleb. It was a much more serious meal than the other times he had been there, but he did his best to be cheerful even though I knew he would miss Caleb almost as much as I would. At the end of the evening he mentioned the square dance on Saturday and asked if eight o'clock was all right. I nodded and glanced at Caleb, but he had turned away.

On the days Caleb was home, we worked on our service for Evaline, gathering material that seemed appropriate — Caleb's knowledge of primitive religions, snatches of prayers or verses from the Bible, poetry. We used whatever we could think of that reflected the rhythms of life that people have always sensed "in the deep heart's core," as the last line of the Yeats poem stated so well.

By the time we were finished, I was again feeling twinges of apprehension about what we were attempting. But I wouldn't back away this time. We had done all we could do. Whether or not it worked, only time would tell.

I treasured those hours spent with Caleb, carefully preserving the memory of them to dwell on after he left. Mother left us alone. Even P.J. seemed to sense we needed privacy, and once again Roger's presence was a blessing in disguise.

On Friday morning Caleb and I walked barefoot along the shore. The tide was out, and we could walk along the water's edge and avoid climbing over rocks. I had brought along an empty mayonnaise jar and stooped at the edge of the shore to fill it with seawater, screwing the cap on tightly.

We walked in silence, letting the yellow foam wash across our feet, squishing strands of wet seaweed with our toes. We stoppped at the point where the curve of the shore disappeared into a wall of craggy boulders that rose from the breaking waves to the lighthouse at the top.

"Let's sit for a while," Caleb said.

We climbed high enough to avoid the blowing spray from the waves and settled ourselves side by side, our backs against a rock. The day was warm but windy, and a parade of puffy clouds dappled the day in light and shadow.

From where we sat, we could see our little sandy beach in the distance and near it the rocks where we had first seen Evaline on the day of Caleb's arrival. I thought of Uncle John, who had appeared twice to Caleb, and wondered if he, too, was still seeking forgiveness.

"If things don't work out in New York," I asked hesitantly, "what will you do then?"

"I'll keep trying elsewhere. For a while, anyway. I have my disability pension. I can get by on not much for quite a while." He tossed a pebble into the waves. "Sooner or later I'll probably go back to school. I had two years of college behind me when I quit to enlist."

"Why did you enlist, Caleb?" I asked after a moment, remembering his encounter with the carnival man.

He gave a short laugh. "It seems so long ago now, I can't even remember. I guess I just felt it was something I needed to do. Maybe it had something to do with Dad and facing things head-on. Wondering whether his suicide was because he had walked away from the life he loved or because he realized too late that perhaps he wasn't talented enough. Wondering if he meant to kill himself at all. . . ." He paused, watching a gull circling overhead. "Or maybe it was getting in touch with something inside me, that place where all the possibilities lie buried, all the 'might bes' instead of the 'might have beens.' ' "

I hesitated again before asking the next question because I knew what his answer would be. But I had to ask it.

"Are we a 'might have been,' Caleb?"

Slowly he stood up and reached down a hand to pull me up after him. He kept hold of my hand, pulling me close to him, and looked at me a long time before answering. "Yes, Molly, as much as we both might wish otherwise, in the way you mean it, we are a 'might have been.' But there can be other 'might bes' ahead for us."

I closed my eyes and said to myself the words he had spoken on the ferry. Maybe someday.

*

That evening, right after supper, while there was still light left, Caleb and I walked out to the cabin. He had promised P.J. a last lesson as soon as we got back, so P.J. didn't plead to come along. We told Mother only that we were going for a final walk. She looked at us with a little frown but made no comment.

I packed a basket with everything we needed, and we took it with us along with Caleb's guitar. The wind had died, and the woods were dark and still. By the time we got to the clearing, only a little twilight still filtered through.

We pushed open the door to the cabin and stepped inside. A feeling of nervous anticipation swept over me. For a moment I hung back in the doorway, then took a deep breath and closed the door behind me.

First I covered the table with a white cloth, then we lit candles, six of them, and arranged them in a semicircle on the table, a half-moon of shimmering light. We had decided on ocean water and the image of the half-moon as symbols for Evaline, the age-old symbols of the feminine. The half-moon was for Evaline the girl, who had lost her childhood too soon, the ocean water for Evaline the woman, who came face-to-face with forces within her she couldn't combat. The warm flicker of the candlelight swept away the shadows that at first had made the cabin uninviting, almost hostile.

I lifted the diary and comb and flint out of the basket and arranged them on the table within the arc of the candles. Caleb propped up the tiny rag doll in the little rocker while I poured the jar of seawater into a small bowl, which I placed on the table with the other objects.

We were ready. Nervously I wiped my palms on my skirt and looked at Caleb.

"I guess we're all set," he said.

He picked up his guitar and went to sit on the edge of the bunk. Softly he began to strum. I listened in silence, thinking of Evaline and the image of her on the beach, of how beautiful she must have been as both a girl and a woman, too. Gradually my nervousness faded. While Caleb played, I began to read from the sheet of paper I held.

"Blessed are they that mourn, for they shall be comforted," I read in a soft voice and then continued our own version of the Sermon on the Mount that we had written for Evaline. "Blessed are they that wander in darkness, for they shall see the light. Blessed are they that seek understanding, for they shall find peace."

I waited a moment, then dipped my fingers into the bowl of seawater and sprinkled the drops across the objects on the table. The candles flickered. I felt a soft stir of air and waited, holding my breath.

I dipped my fingers into the bowl again and this time sprinkled the water on the doll in the rocker. The candles flickered, and again I caught my breath. Evaline was with us, I was sure.

Caleb's fingers moved lightly over the strings of the guitar. The music, too, was comforting.

I turned to my paper again and read the passage we had written, loosely based on lines from the Book of Revelation. "Where you are, there shall be no night. And you shall need neither candle nor the light of the sun. For you shall have eternal light and peace everlasting."

I picked up the bowl of water and slowly circled the room, dipping my fingers into the water, sprinkling the drops to the left and to the right of me as I made my way around the small space. As I passed Caleb, some of the drops of water fell on him. He looked at me, his eyes dark and serious.

When I completed the circle, I set the bowl back on the table. Although we hadn't planned it that way, something made me go to the rocker and pick up the doll. I held it in the crook of my arm, rocking it gently back and forth. Then I read the last of the part Caleb and I had written, and I thought of Letitia Hornsby. Someday soon I would go and tell her we had given Evaline her message.

"Evaline Bloodsworth, you are forgiven for all the sins that trouble you. May you be granted eternal rest. May perpetual light shine on you. May your soul be freed from torment and from the waters of darkness, and may light and grace shine on you."

Softly, Caleb began to sing. The words were an old Gaelic blessing that he had set to his own music. I listened as he sang it there in the cabin in the candlelight.

> *Deep peace of the running wave to you*
> *Deep peace of the flowing air to you*
> *Deep peace of the quiet earth to you.*

He paused, now only humming the melody. I looked at the candles. The flames were still. At my back I felt a stir of air like the touch of a moth's wing across the back of my neck. Nothing more than that. Carefully I placed the doll back in the rocker and knelt beside it near the edge of the bunk.

Caleb began to sing again, and I turned my attention to him.

> *Deep peace of the shining stars to you*
> *Deep peace of the gentle night to you*
> *Moon and stars pour their healing light on you*
> *Deep peace to you.*

When he came to the last phrase, he started again, singing it through a second time. The soft light, the melody, the sound of his voice, the repetition of the words *deep peace* — all soothed me, almost mesmerized me as though I were in twilight sleep.

At the very end, Caleb repeated "deep peace to you" slowly over and over, as though he, too, were in a trance. But his face was drawn and tense, his eyes closed. His voice died. Slowly he laid the guitar on the bunk beside him.

We had finished. We had done for Evaline all we could do. I had kept my promise.

I looked at Caleb and saw it wasn't enough. Something was incomplete. And suddenly I knew this hadn't been just for Evaline. It was for all of us. For myself. For Mother and most certainly for my father. For Uncle John. For Caleb. Especially for Caleb.

Very quietly I began to sing the words I still remembered so well, sang by myself in the stillness of the cabin.

> *Amazing grace, how sweet the sound*
> *That saved a wretch like me,*
> *I once was lost but now am found,*
> *Was blind but now I see.*

I looked at Caleb and my voice faltered.

"Sing with me, Caleb," I whispered and then I began again.

By the time I came to the end of the first line, Caleb had joined me, and together we sang the rest of the verse, my soprano carrying the melody while his tenor sang the harmony. Caleb's head was bent, his face in shadow.

> *I once was lost but now am found,*
> *Was blind but now I see.*

I began the third verse, and Caleb stayed with me.

> *Through many dangers, toils, and snares*
> *I have already come,*
> *'Tis grace that brought me safe thus far,*
> *And grace will lead me home.*

Our voices held the last *home*. Gradually they faded. The cabin was silent, the candles no longer flickered.

Caleb raised his head. His cheeks were wet and glistened in the candlelight. Tears ran down his face, and he made no move to check them.

In an instant I was across the space that separated us, kneeling beside him on the edge of the bunk. His arms circled me. His hands pressed hard against my back. My arms went around him and I held him, hugging him with all the strength

I had. I held him, my child, my lover, my cousin Caleb, until all his tears were spent.

When at last I looked up, the chair was rocking slowly back and forth, and it was empty. The doll was gone. I breathed a long sigh of relief.

*

The next morning, Mother said good-bye to Caleb at the house and made P.J. do the same. She let me drive Caleb by myself to Bucks Harbor to catch the first ferry to the mainland.

We didn't arrive at the ferry until almost time for it to depart. Neither of us wanted to prolong the moment of saying good-bye. In silence we walked down the dock much as we had the day he arrived, Caleb carrying his duffel and I the guitar, but now he had put aside his cane and no longer used it. I also carried my drawing, rolled loosely and secured with a piece of yarn.

I thought back to the morning of his arrival, when the ferry appeared out of the mist like some ghost ship and a dark, brooding look shadowed his face as he waited to step off the ferry. Nothing that day had prepared me for what was coming or the changes that would take place in both of us.

Today, instead of being shrouded in mist, the ferry waited at the end of the pier in bright sunlight. The water sparkled.

At the far end of the pier, Caleb set down his duffel. The ferry was crowded with summer people day-tripping to the mainland, but they had already boarded and the dock was almost empty. We stood by the gangplank, face-to-face.

I looked at Caleb. Today he, too, was washed with light.

I handed him the drawing. "I would've had it framed for

you," I said, "but I thought it would be too awkward to carry." My voice shook.

He slid the yarn from the drawing and unrolled it. I held one side, and he held the other so that he could see the whole picture. I looked at it with him, trying to see it through his eyes.

I had placed Caleb in the center, seated on a stool, holding his guitar, one side of his face in light, the other in shadow. He was the largest figure in the drawing and dominated it, but around him I had drawn a series of smaller pictures, each one separate — his old house, the schooner *Innisfree,* the framed photo on his dresser of him and Uncle John, a lobster pot and a fish on a line, the cabin hidden in a grove of pine trees, and, finally, at his left side, I had drawn myself in front of an easel, at work on this drawing.

He looked at it until the ferry startled us both with a loud blast of its horn. Slowly he rolled up the drawing, slipped on the yarn tie, and carefully set it on top of his duffel. Then he pulled me to him, pressing his cheek against mine, his arms wrapped around me.

"Molly, Molly," he whispered. "What a wonderful gift this is. But you were the best gift of all, one I never dreamed I would find here."

I couldn't let go of him.

The horn blasted twice, the signal that the gangplank was about to go up.

"I have a gift for you, too," he said softly in my ear. "You'll hear it this afternoon on the radio. I wrote it for you."

I couldn't speak. I just nodded.

"You gettin' on, buddy?" one of the dockhands called out. "We're taking up the gangplank."

Slowly Caleb stepped back. He picked up the duffel and his guitar, crossed the gangplank onto the ferry, and disappeared behind the crowd that lined the rail.

Somehow I got to the car and almost home. As I drove slowly around the curve at High Point, something in the ocean caught my eye. Whether it was a white sail in the distance, or just the glint of the sun off a whitecap, I couldn't be sure. But I pulled off the road and parked the Jeep in the same spot I had parked when I brought Caleb home. I walked to the edge of the cliff and looked down at the rocks where we had first seen that ghostly figure of a girl. I imagined her holding the doll in her arms. You can sleep now, Evaline, I thought.

And Caleb, too, I hoped. No more nightmares, no more brooding about Uncle John's suicide and wondering whether he, too, could feel such despair. He had made me a promise last night before we left the cabin, and I knew he would keep it.

I also knew that we can't turn our backs on what we long for most. It was going to be especially hard not to long for Caleb. But no matter what else happened, I would never turn my back on him. The feeling of affinity that had brought us together would always be there, for me as well as for him. It would sustain me when I needed it most, for whatever lay ahead.

Chiaroscuro. The word still rolled off my tongue, and maybe someday I really would be known as Molly Todd, the famous chiaroscurist. That would be enough.

Shielding my eyes against the sun, I looked out across the water. Below, on such a clear day, the green sea glistened like Caleb's eyes.